THY KING DUMB COME

THY KING DUMB COME

STEPHEN TRYON

AccountabilityCitizenship.org

Publisher's Cataloging-In-Publication Data
(Prepared by The Donohue Group, Inc.)

Names: Tryon, Stephen, author.
Title: Thy King Dumb come / Stephen Tryon.
Description: [Salt Lake City, Utah] : [AccountabilityCitizenship.org],
    [2021] | A parody of contemporary American politics.
Identifiers: ISBN 9781734304749 (paperback) | ISBN 9781734304732
    (ebook)
Subjects: LCSH: United States--Politics and government--Fiction. |
    Presidents--United States--Fiction. | Kings and rulers--Fiction. |
    Students--Fiction. | Dreams--Fiction.
    Philosophers--Fiction. | LCGFT: Parodies (Literature)
Classification: LCC PS3620.R96 T49 2021 (print) | LCC PS3620.R96 (ebook)
    | DDC 813/.6--dc23

Library of Congress Control Number: 2020916542

"What cracker is this same, that deafs our ears with this abundance
of superfluous breath?"
William Shakespeare, King John (II:1:147)

For my mom, who taught me how to pray.

CONTENTS

CHAPTER 1

A Dream Within A Dream

It had been a long day.

I was closing in on the final four weeks of my masters program, and pushing hard to keep up with reading and polishing final projects. Saturdays were precious, because I could focus only on coursework. During the week, the job kept me busy by day, limiting my study time to the evenings.

Mornings have always been the most efficient part of my day. So I tried to attack the hardest material then. This Saturday morning, I had plowed through chapters on the latest machine models used to crunch and analyze massive data sets. The material fascinated me; it seemed related to the decision theory and epistemology I had studied enroute to my first masters thirty years earlier. Now, the techniques for building machine models seemed to offer a fresh and promising way of understanding how we can know something is true.

When my mind grew tired, I would take breaks. These consisted either of short naps or snack breaks in front of the television. The naps were the best, but risky—I sometimes found I lost too much of the day. Snack breaks were less risky, but also not quite as refreshing, especially since most of the television I watched was news coverage of the incessant controversy surrounding the president.

Today I had watched an evangelical Christian explaining away the moral shortfalls of President Donny Dumb by citing Dumb's steadfast support for conservative judges. It seemed to me that many American Christians had been deceived into supporting Dumb by a cynical distortion of the main message Jesus taught in the Gospels.

Populist religious figures, more political power brokers than true Christians, subordinated the precept of 'love your neighbor as yourself' to messages they could sell to both the masses and to political elites. I was shocked at how easily many Christians were deceived. For the evangelical I saw interviewed, it all came down to abortion—nothing else mattered.

On my last break earlier in the evening, medical experts were contrasting the American government's slow response to the current pandemic with the response of the South Korean government, concluding that the president's refusal to pay attention to intelligence reports in early January had caused thousands more Americans to die than would have if he had followed the Korean example.

I worked hard to keep an open mind on the political stuff. We all have biases, I know, and those biases shape our views in imperceptible ways. I had, therefore, long ago taken to heart the wisdom of Socrates —that the path to knowledge begins with the acceptance of one's own ignorance and the honest consideration of alternative views. It had always seemed to me that the master virtue of our republic should be tolerance, and our institutions should be built for compromise rather than the ceaseless power struggle between this party and that party that seemed to dominate the news.

Now I was tired, and my eyes hurt. I thought I could maybe push for another hour before the fatigue forced me to go to bed. And I was almost done with the cyber security lab I had set as my final goal for tonight.

I rubbed my eyes and blinked at the picture of the chocolate lab that had died a few months previously. "What do you say, Peanut?," I muttered to myself. "Once more unto the breach?" Maybe I'll just put my head down and close my eyes for a few minutes before I hit this last section, I thought.

Donnie Dumb

I could tell I was dreaming.

I was flying, buffeted by strong currents of air that seemed to come from nowhere. Slightly disoriented, I spotted a brown ledge and willed myself to glide in that direction. There was an odd feeling in my arms, as if they were connected to my legs with a sheet-like material that caught air, slowing my momentum as I glided effortlessly onto the ledge. From the reflection in the glass wall adjacent to where I landed, I was surprised to see I was a moth.

The ledge I landed on was the heavy frame of one of the portraits adorning the walls of a large office. A group of people sat on two white couches and some chairs flanking a long coffee table near the center of the room. The Great Seal of the United States was emblazoned on a rug midway between the coffee table and a large wooden desk.

I realized immediately that one advantage of being a person dreaming I was a moth is that I could understand what the people were saying. I wondered if all moths could understand people. The sound waves set up a vibration in the glass within the frame, so I could hear clearly, like home theater.

President Donnie Dumb spoke angrily in a voice I recognized from the 6 o'clock news.

"Why do they keep blaming me for the virus? You all aren't doing your jobs! You're supposed to be emphasizing that the virus came from China, and that things would be much worse if I had not acted to shut down travel from China. I don't understand why my poll numbers keep dropping."

Sir, we have been emphasizing that chronology," an aide said. "But the Korea example is gaining traction from this May editorial out of Salt Lake City. It turns out Korea had their first reported case of coronavirus on the same day we had ours. But they started very aggressive testing, contact tracing and isolation protocols almost immediately. We waited almost eight weeks before beginning to do things the Koreans started doing right away. According to this editorial, that delay is the reason Americans are 21 times more likely to catch coronavirus and 60 times more likely to die from it than South Koreans are."

"Fake news! Let me tweet that!" He pulled up his phone and hammered away with short, pudgy fingers. Looking back up, he turned to his press secretary. "You're failing me on this!"

The other aide continued talking about the editorial. "The problem is that the facts in the editorial correspond with facts on the ground in South Korea. That correspondence and independent verifiability are what people traditionally use to determine the difference between the truth and fake news. Millions of Americans were watching Korean professional baseball on television in May, while our leagues didn't even started playing games until July."

"Correspondence and verifiability? Those are bad words, and bad people use them. I have better words. The best words, some people say. Other people, not me. I like 'reciprossssity.' One of my favorite words. Reciprosity is what makes the mob... work." He turned to his press secretary. "I want you to reach out to our Fox friends. I want them, and you, to start emphasizing my chronology. I want you to start emphasizing that we can't trust numbers from South Korea. And I want you to do that right away!"

"Yes, Mr. President," the young woman replied, rising and bustling out of the room.

Turning back to the other aides seated with him, he continued. "That ought to help the poll numbers. As long as we can get an alternative story out there, we can confuse things enough so our base will stay with us."

"God, I wish I didn't have to worry about the poll numbers and the fake news from the fake news media." He glared at his Chief of Staff. "What do you think? What can you do to help me with the polls?"

I could not see the Chief of Staff's face, and frankly had lost track of which one this was. Launching myself from the frame, I fluttered through turbulent space, over the great seal, over the large wooden desk, coming to rest on a white ledge embedded in a semicircle of windows that looked out on an expanse of green grass.

Now I could see his face as he droned on in response to the president's question. "...the news drives polls here in the United States. So I think your strategy is brilliant, Mr. President. I'm not sure there's any other solution to the poll problem. If I were king, I would snap my fingers and stop all the negative press, but I'm afraid I can't do that."

"Wait a minute! That's a great idea, Paul. YOU can't do that, but what about ME? What if I could be king? Then I could snap my fingers." He tried to do that, but his fingers were so short and pudgy that they made a small rubbing sound, more like caterpillar wings than a real snap. "Could I sign an executive order making myself king?"

"I'm pretty sure that's illegal, Mr. President." This from the aide that had brought up the editorial from the Salt Lake Tribune. "I mean, the Constitution gives you specified powers, but I'm pretty sure making yourself king is not one of them."

"You should go check on that," the president said to the aide. "Now! And don't mention it to anybody. Report what you find out to Paul." The aide rose and left the room, leaving the president alone with Paul Pasturepie, his Chief of Staff.

"Who is that? He's a pretty negative boy. Don't bring him back, okay? I don't have time for Negative Nancies."

"Yes, Mr. President," Pasturepie said. "He does have a point about the law, though. I'm afraid there would be quite a backlash if you tried to make yourself king."

"You worry too much about the law. That's the Attorney Gerbil's job. I used to have to worry about law, but that was only when I had Senator Recuse-My-Face as Attorney Gerbil. I fixed that problem."

"If you say so, Mr. President."

"I do say so. Let's get the Attorney Gerbil on the phone... better yet have him come over for a face-to-face right away. Just you, me and him. Top priority. No negative boys. Keep this hush-hush until we figure it out."

Suddenly a large shadow hurtled into the glass next to my head with a loud thud, startling me out of my dream.

Socrates

I awoke with a jolt, the bright sunlight and the smell of fresh-cut grass surprising and confusing me. Two large, liquid eyes stared at me from their perch above and behind a wet, black nose and an expanse of brown fur and gray whiskers that began just a few inches in front of my own nose. The creature had obviously been studying me as I slept.

"Peanut?"

"Who's Peanut? Not me. Who are you, anyway? You've been laying on my toy, you know." The dog enunciated each word with deep, melodious precision.

I noticed for the first time the smell of rubber and the worn, 12-inch oblong cylinder, green and off-white, streaked with grass and mud stains. My right hand was still wrapped around one end of the toy. The other end had been resting under my head. I had pushed myself halfway to a seated position on the grass, from where I had been laying on my left side. At least I wasn't a moth anymore.

"Oh, sorry," I said, pushing myself the rest of the way up. I extended the hand with the toy toward the dog, who reached forward from the neck, without moving his body, and took the cylinder in his mouth. He lowered his head and dropped the toy onto the grass between his front paws, then raised his head again, cocking it slightly to one side and eying me curiously.

"Apology accepted. It's nice to see that some of you people still have manners. But you really shouldn't go around sleeping in other creature's yards and using their stuff for your pillow. Is that part of your model?"

"Wait, who are you? Are you sure you aren't Peanut? He had a toy just like that. And how can you talk?"

"That is a lot of questions. I am not Peanut. I am Socrates. The fact that Peanut had a toy that looked like mine is not sufficient evidence for you to keep trying to make me someone I am not, so please stop that. And I speak for the same reason you do—social animals have to communicate with other social animals. It's part of our major model."

"What's all this talk about models?," I said, scratching my head.

"What universe are you from? Models are everything. Not everyone knows what their model is, or rather, what their models are, but everyone has models. Life is impossible without them."

"So you are a social animal, and therefore you act in accordance with a social animal model?"

"Yes."

"But you're a dog. Peanut was a dog, and he didn't talk. And he looked just like you."

"Stop it! The fact that—to you—Peanut looked like me—is irrelevant. Next thing you know, you will be telling me that all us dogs look alike to you. What are you, some kind of Republican? And the fact that your Peanut never chose to speak to you does NOT mean that Peanut could not speak. In fact, if I could go back in time 15 minutes, I would choose not to speak to you as well. It's quite frustrating."

"I AM sorry, but this is all rather extraordinary to me. You ARE a dog, after all, and where I am from, dogs are not rational, and do not speak. You are acting like a person."

"Hold your tongue. People are no more rational than any other creature with a rational capacity, and in my experience, most people choose custom and superstition over rationality. And the fact that most people choose to speak just enables them to spread their ignorance like a virus. Saying I am acting like a person is an insult."

"I didn't MEAN to insult you. It's just this is all very different..."

"... I know, I know, from where you are from. Which raises an interesting point—where are you from, exactly, and how did you get into my yard?"

"EXACTLY IS RIGHT!" A shrill voice ca-cawed from a tree branch, and at almost the same instant a dark shadow passed quickly overhead and a large black bird landed just a few feet away. "I've been listening the whole time, young man, so you'd better answer up if you know what's good for you."

The ICE Raven

"Oh great, does every creature here speak? Who are you?"

"I'll ask the questions here. I've been listening, and you sound like you come from somewhere else. Are you an illegal alien?"

"Oh, come on, Raven," Socrates intoned, "Give the kid a chance, will you? He's just confused. He was just about to tell me where he's from." He looked at me expectantly.

"No, I'm not here illegally," I stammered. "I mean, I'm not exactly sure where 'here' is. I was working in my house, and I just closed my eyes for a few minutes, and I woke up here." I thought it unwise to mention eavesdropping on the President. "But I am an American."

"That doesn't tell me much," snapped the bird. "There are an awful lot of kool-aid-drinking liberals around here who call themselves Americans. Do you support sanctuary cities or King and Country? That's what I want to know."

"Americans don't have a king, that is one thing I know. If you are asking whether I support President Dumb, then the answer is no. I think he has been criminally negligent in his failure to effectively use the resources of the federal government to respond to the virus. I think his negligence has been intentional, to advance his own political interests at the expense of the people of the United States. Who are you, anyway?" Turning to Socrates, he repeated, "Who is this?"

"This," Socrates sighed, "is an ICE raven."

"I thought ravens were warm-weather birds."

"No, ICE is the government organization they serve. They were originally intended to help secure our borders after the attack by Islamic terrorists, but those waters have gotten a bit muddy. Now you find them flocking around all over the country trying to enforce customs and immigration laws. A thankless and dangerous job, to be sure, and it attracts some interesting creatures."

"Well, birds of a feather flock together, they say."

"They do? I have never heard that," the raven interjected, "and I don't like the way you said it, either. I don't like the way you talk about our President. You talk like a traitor Democrat. Are you saved?"

"Am I in danger?"

"Ah ha! Just as I suspected. A liberal, smart-aleck. Not a Christian, are you? Christians are saved by Jesus Christ. And ours is a Christian kingdom."

"You keep talking about a kingdom. Is this America, or isn't it? It isn't a kingdom. We don't have a king. And while we have a strong history as a majority Christian nation, our country was founded on religious tolerance. At least two of the first three presidents were not Christians at all, you know."

"You liar! And you are being disrespectful to our customs, so as an officer charged to enforce customs, I am writing you a citation. You will have to appear in court. And you better get your story straight before then. The judge knows how to handle snowflakes. And we've just about replaced all the liberal judges!"

"I don't think those are the kinds of customs..."

"Silence!" shrieked the raven, pen in beak and pad propped against a rock. "What's your name?"

"Stephen."

"Very well. I'll see you in court in three days. THREE DAYS. You'd better be there, or you'll be in a whole lot worse trouble." The raven tore the citation from the pad and dropped it at my feet, then gathered his things and flew off.

"Oh, my, I AM sorry about that," Socrates said. "This is big trouble."

"Really? Can't I just pay a fine or something?"

"No, I am afraid not. You will have to appear in court. And the cross examinations can be pretty grueling. They all seem to take being right, or at least not being shown to be wrong, quite seriously."

"Okay, well, maybe I can get back to my house before then. What do you think I should do to find my way home?"

"I do not know. It would be reckless of me to guess, since I do not know how you got here. But I think it would be wise for us to pay a visit to the model-makers' workshop. The model makers can help you understand your models, and that might help us figure out how you came to be here. It will certainly help you answer any questions the judge has for you, if it comes to that."

"How do I find the model makers?"

"I'll take you to them. Follow me."

A Walk In The Woods

Socrates pushed himself to his feet and sauntered towards a cathedral-shaped gate in a white, wooden fence about 20 yards away. I trailed along behind him. He reared up on his hind legs and hit the latch with his paws, and the gate flew open. I pushed the gate closed behind me and followed as Socrates led the way across a manicured lawn, skirting the fence line until it ended. Then he headed off to the left, following a little trail into the woods.

It was quiet, I thought as I followed. "Hey, where are all the people?"

"The people are all quarantining to avoid the virus. And that reminds me, why aren't you wearing a mask? Are you a Republican?"

"I wear a mask when I go places where there are other people. They are supposed to help protect others from any germs I might spread, you know. But I really wasn't expecting to be outside. I just closed my eyes for a minute and woke up with you. I don't know how I got here."

"Yeah, you keep saying that. We have to do something about your story. That line isn't going to play well in court. Makes you sound like Bill Cosby's last date. But we have some time. It will take us a while to get to the model makers. And I have an idea."

"What's your idea?"

"Well, you know, starting an inquiry or a conversation by admitting that you don't know anything at all about the subject is not a bad first move. I do it all the time. It's kind of my schtick."

"Really?"

"Yeah. And then I follow up by inviting my audience to join me in exploring the issue at hand, contributing their views and challenging my assertions until we reach agreement on a conclusion. That way, we often all can agree on what we know. But that is all a product of the process of inquiry that starts with me admitting I know nothing. The others have to at least be willing to participate in an honest examination of what they claim to know."

"Interesting. So it works sometimes, and sometimes it doesn't?"

"Yes, that is correct. I can usually bring people to the conclusion I want, but sometimes it doesn't work. I was speaking with a young coyote named Callicles the other day. I simply could not get him to agree to a logical definition of virtue. Quite frustrating."

"Do you use the same process every time? Can you identify any characteristics that seem to generate successful dialogues versus the unsuccessful ones?

"Well, I am always trying to establish common ground at first, so that often means I start with a definition or real-life example of a familiar concept or class of things, and then I try to establish a connection to another concept or class of things. I try to make that connection using common experience or practice so that I am persuasive. I am practicing the art of rhetoric."

"Why do you think it didn't work with virtue? It does seem like there should be some pretty broad agreement on what that looks like."

"Yes, I have no trouble getting people to agree on what it looks like. But Callicles, and apparently a bunch of other people as well, think the best virtue is to appear virtuous while, at the same time secretly using the appearance of virtue as a mask for whatever behavior you need to practice to become rich and powerful, even if that behavior is not virtuous at all. I think that kind of behavior is, at least, horribly hypocritical and clearly not virtue."

"And I would agree."

"But if the hypocrisy is never discovered, or if at least it is not discovered until no one has the power to hold the hypocrite accountable,

Callicles seems to think there is no way to differentiate that behavior from what I would call true virtue.

He points out that I argue for the importance of virtue based on it being necessary for a cohesive society and for the happiness that virtue brings to the virtuous person. And he concludes that the appearance of virtue would serve just as well, and the guarantee of wealth and power will make a person happier than the intangible feeling of true virtue. I am certainly not convinced of his position, but neither is he moved by my argument. And there seems to be quite a number of people who agree with Callicles."

"So it would seem that you disagree about the meaning of virtue itself, and therefore cannot use that concept as a premise in an argument to find agreement about how people should conduct themselves. Interesting."

"How do you account for the cases where you are successful?," I continued. "There are differences between individual ideas on the meaning of other concepts as well, right?"

"That is true. But in cases where I succeed in convincing my audience, there is some discernible benefit to resolving differences in individual perception. If I am standing to the east of a large, irregularly-shaped rock the size of a building, and you are standing to the north of it, your idea of what it looks like will be different from mine. Sometimes, it is better for all of us to overcome the differences in our many different perspectives on what the rock looks like to get the most accurate description of the rock."

"Also, with some things, there are external cues that help us differentiate more accurate perceptions from less accurate perceptions. With this killer virus, for instance, President Dumb's assertions that it was 'just the flu' and that it would 'just disappear' are clearly wrong."

"The perceptions of people who warned that the virus was more deadly than the flu, and that we needed a coherent national strategy, were more accurate. We have external cues that confirm this for us: the number of Americans who are still dying from the virus every day, and the example of countries with coherent national strategies."

"Ah, I see. In the case of virtue, there may be no external cues to help us differentiate between someone who is truly virtuous and someone who is good at deceiving others by projecting a false image of virtue."

The path they were following reached a fork in front of a large oak. Pointed wooden signs nailed to the tree informed the travelers that an incline to the left would take them to Arete Pasteur. I wondered if someone had misspelled 'Pasture' or if the left fork really went to a place called Arete Pasteur. Before I could ask, Socrates took the right fork, which zig-zagged up a steep, wooded incline. The tree-sign told me we were heading toward Overfit Orchard.

"It's too bad there isn't a way to give people a definitive sense of what virtue is, almost like a picture of the real shape of that rock you were talking about," I puffed heavily as we climbed the hill.

"Funny you should say that. I have a friend, a bright young lab, who has some ideas along those lines. In fact, that's him now up ahead."

Cresting the hill, I noticed we had entered a grove thick with apple and cherry trees in full blossom. A light-boned, young black lab-boxer mix caught sight of them and raced over to Socrates, pouncing into a crouch and wagging his tail and barking playfully. Socrates lowered his head and pushed against the side of the young dog's head with his gray muzzle. A low-toned series of short, playful woofs tumbled from somewhere deep in the older dog's chest.

"Stephen, meet Plato."

Plato's Ideas

"Hello. Am I picking up a heavy Classical Greek vibe, or is it just me?"

"Yo dawg. Socrates is the classical one. I like to think of myself as a bit more contemporary, if you know what I mean. And what about you? Stephen—one of the original stoners, right? You like a little puff-the-magic-dragon? I might hook you up?"

"Ha! Well, I was named for a priest who was named for a guy... who got stoned, but I don't think in the sense of puff-the-magic-dragon.

Things are weird enough for me at the moment. I had better just stick with Socrates' plan and talk to the model makers."

"Is Descartes around, Plato?" Socrates interjected.

"Right! Yeah, come on with me. I saw him over by the pond a few minutes ago." Plato bounced off across the hilltop in the direction from which he had come. "This way!" he called over his shoulder.

Following the young dog through the bright grove of trees, I noticed a cacophony of animal noises all around. Birds and squirrels and rabbits clustered all about in small groups, chattering and chirping merrily. After sixty or seventy yards, the ground dropped off in a gentle incline, and they emerged into a brightly lit clearing dominated by a ragged oval-shaped pond of murky green water. A large raccoon sat on a log by the water's edge, puffing a pipe.

"Hey, Descartes! Socrates is here, with a guest. What are you smoking, my friend? Some of that nice stuff I brought you from the pasteur?" .

"Hi, Plato, yes, that was thoughtful of you. Hey there, Socrates, what brings you into the woods?" He smiled and waved a big paw at me in acknowledgement as he spoke.

"Well, my new friend Stephen here found himself waking up on the grass outside my doghouse, and doesn't really know how he got there. An ICE raven heard him as he was explaining that to me, and wrote him a citation for undermining our customs. So he has to appear in court in a few days. I thought a talk with some model makers might help him understand where he came from and how to get back there. And even if he can't get back there, I thought you all could help prepare him for his court appearance."

"Ah, perhaps we can help. He should start down at the pasteur, though. Maybe Plato can take him? I could use your help here with some challenges we are facing with the federal models. The foxes have really made a mess of things."

"That works for me. Plato, I told Stephen he should talk to you about your Ideas and how to get past the different perceptions we all seem to have about some things. Then, could you take him to the pasteur to see Aristotle?"

"Sure, I can do that. But you be careful with the foxes. They have bad purposes in mind for you. Come on this way, Stephen." Plato led off toward a new path that rose slightly from the pond rounding the hill they had come down, without returning to the summit. Stopping at the edge of the clearing, he barked sternly back at the raccoon and the brown lab. "You take care of him, D!"

A combination of low growl and whine escaped Plato's muzzle as he turned back to the path, obviously none too pleased to be leaving Socrates.

"Thank you for taking me to the pasteur," I said. "I'm sorry to be taking you away from Socrates."

"Oh, that is okay. It's just those damned foxes are up to no good. Socrates is in danger and he is too naïve to know it. That's really the whole reason I came up with my doctrine of Ideas in the first place."

"Really? He was talking about how we all have different perspectives, and was using the metaphor of an enormous rock that appears to have a different shape depending on the direction from which a person is viewing it. I mentioned how nice it would be to have a god's eye view of the rock we could all share, and that's when he said I should talk to you."

Yeah, that makes sense. Socrates is brilliant. His notion of starting with humility as a rhetorical way to encourage consensus is exactly the right approach, in a perfect world. If everyone was willing to honestly acknowledge that none of our individual solutions are as good as the best solution we come up with together, that would be a great society. But the whole system really depends on acceptance of the notion that we are social animals, and then grounding the definition of virtue on that foundation."

"The foxes consistently preach that true virtue is self interest. Self interest is certainly a legitimate decision criterion for each of us, but virtue is a social concept, and in society, self interest should be subordinate to achieving the best consensus—the consensus that best balances the individual self interest of each with the collective good of all. The fox network spreads the lie that we all should just look out for ourselves, and that the appearance of social virtue is just another facet of self interest. They cloak their ambition with colorful words about the glory of the state and the glory of God. That message is popular in some circles. I fear they will find a way to turn the people's hearts against Socrates so they can get him out of their way."

"So the acceptance of our nature as social animals is key, and the social definition of virtue follows from that. Socrates mentioned a young coyote who recently refused to accept either premise," I remarked.

"Callicles!" Plato growled. "He is one of the bad ones."

"Socrates said you had ideas about providing a common perception of concepts like virtue, about which there is some disagreement?"

"Yes. To defend Socrates, and his legacy, we have to give a metaphysical reality to concepts like virtue. You know, Socrates' metaphor of the rock is powerful because we all have experience of large rocks and certain of their properties are beyond question. If you were to walk up to the exposed rock face of a cliff on the side of a mountain, for instance, you would know that you could not simply walk through the rock. So those kinds of attributes of rocks, and of other things that are certain, are things that Socrates uses to his advantage in his rhetoric, using them to make deductions about the properties of other things. My doctrine of Ideas is an attempt to make all Ideas like Socrates' rock."

"Yes, I see what you mean."

"It is only on things like virtue, where the foxes are able to call reality into doubt, that Socrates' arguments stumble. But there is enough disagreement between our individual perceptions and sense experiences to make that quite a challenge."

"Well," I interrupted, "in my world science has established the physical mechanisms that underlie a great deal of what we observe in the world around us, and why perceptions differ. But I understand that was not yet the case in Plato's time, so go on."

"Ok, in my time, before your science, I simply observed that our different perceptions about things are an obstacle to building a just society. None of our perceptions are, as you say, the god's-eye view. I solve this problem by placing the god's-eye view of everything into a metaphysical realm of Ideas. It is only the Ideas that are real in the sense of Socrates' rock. There is an Idea of Socrates' rock, and an Idea of virtue. Our experience of these things in our lives is simply a distorted perception of the real Idea of those things. We can, through our reason, gain true knowledge of the reality of a thing like the Idea of virtue. But this is difficult, and most people never achieve it."

"Well, I understand why you are attempting to establish this idea of a metaphysical realm of Ideas, but isn't it just as easy for people to deny your metaphysical Idea of virtue as it is for Callicles to refuse to accept Socrates' definition of virtue? After all, yours is a system that tells people that all they see and touch and taste is a distorted illusion and that the only true reality can be known only with reason. It seems anyone could claim to have the best insight into your metaphysical realm of Ideas."

"Perhaps. And if you are familiar with my Republic, then you know that I address that criticism by proposing a perfect society ruled by benevolent philosopher kings, chosen and trained throughout their lifetime to build their reason so they could guide the other classes of people with their experience of the realm of ideas."

"I am familiar with Republic. It is a pretty scary vision, frankly, without much of the freedom we are used to in my world. It seems like too great a price to pay to gain a unanimous consensus on the content of the concept of virtue."

"Perhaps. But in my experience—and I think Socrates agrees with me—the way that preserves your freedom makes it very difficult to control the foxes."

"Do you mind if I ask what happened to Plato the hip? You were talking like a rapper when we first met, and now you've adopted a different manner."

"Really? Arc you sure I was talking differently, or were you just hearing me differently because of my appearance? From my perspective, I wasn't speaking any differently then than I am now. Check your cognitive bias, my friend. Black Labs Matter!"

As he said this, the path they were following emerged from the woods into a lush green pasture. A large, noble stallion the color of chestnuts raised his head from where he was munching a clump of clover. Head held high, he started to a trot, heading in their direction.

"That is Aristotle," Plato said.

Aristotle

"Hello, Plato. To what do I owe the privilege of a visit from my old teacher?" Then, turning his broad, intelligent face in my direction, "And good day to you, sir. My name is Aristotle."

Plato responded, "Hello, Aristotle. This is Stephen, a human Socrates found asleep outside his doghouse this morning. He got in a bit of trouble with an ICE raven and will have to appear in court in a few days. Socrates brought him to Descartes for some help getting ready, and Descartes asked me to bring him to speak with you first."

"That was a wise choice. Socrates should know better than to put Descartes before the horse!" the stallion chuckled. And then, turning to me again, "How did you come to be sleeping on Socrates' doorstep?"

"I honestly don't know. I was studying in my house. It was late. I was tired, and put my head down for a second, and woke up here. And frankly, this seems a long way from where I was before. Where I came from, the animals don't talk. Some things are the same, though. The politics, if I understand them correctly, and the virus situation are familiar to me. Anyway, Socrates thought speaking with model-makers might help me remember how to get home, or at least prepare me for my court appearance."

"Ah, good thinking there. And I suppose he and Plato have conveyed the foundations of their philosophies, and of mine as well—that humans are social animals like dogs and horses?"

"Yes."

"And the fundamental importance of humility—acknowledging that our individual perspectives are imperfect and seeking to join the wisdom of others with our own in pursuit of the truth?"

"That, too."

"Very well. As a broad generalization, we can say that Socrates relied on deduction from concepts based on common experience and practice. He ran into difficulties with people who proposed counterexamples to his concepts of virtue, the good, and social animals—counterexamples which we must concede are consistent with some degree of experience, although we might not think they represent the best of our natures. Perhaps to defend his teacher's views, Plato, here, proposed that reality lies in a realm of Ideas inaccessible by experience. His Ideas are accessible only through reason, and align with the concepts as Socrates proposed them. Plato even thought to propose a way to protect his immutable Ideas from corruption, by making them accessible only to the very few who could perfect their reason. These few, Plato argues, should therefore be the philosopher kings who should rule the ideal human society."

"Well stated, my friend. But as much as I am glad if my Ideas help defend Socrates, they are simply the way I think reality must be, if we are to account for the imperfections of experience."

"But through no fault of yours or Socrates, your theories can be refuted by those who offer their own models. With no science to arbitrate for the truth, we are left with a confusing array of conflicting theories. That challenge led me in a different direction. I use our individual experience—with all its imperfections—as a way of marshaling evidence in support of the truth."

"My model is fundamentally inductive rather than deductive. I use all of the individual cases of any given species that I can observe. From these observations, I derive a set of general characteristics inclusive of the naturally occurring variations we find in the population over time. My use of observations is an early step toward the scientific method. Inductive reasoning allows us to use counterexamples to build more powerful theories, and..."

Aristotle was interrupted by the loud chorus of a flock of small birds that darted toward them, flitting from tree to tree around the circumference of the field. They perched nearby, like students wanting to hear Aristotle's dissertation, but the sound of their singing drowned out his voice. I noticed the songs were slightly different. Some seemed to be crying "Heat the liquid, kill the germs! Heat the liquid, kill the germs!", while others sounded more like "Vaccinate! Vaccinate!"

"Oh, my, that is loud!" Aristotle neighed. "Let's move this way a bit," trotting along the edge of the field in the direction from which the birds had come. "They are looking for food. I doubt they will backtrack." Sure enough, the sound of the birds subsided as the distance between the flock and the philosopher grew.

"That was odd," I remarked, "Did you hear what they were singing?"

"Just the normal songs of the Pasteur Sparrow," Aristotle replied. "The founder of that model, Louis, was a pioneer in using scientific methods to fight disease. You people are using a lot of his ideas to fight this virus of yours. Now, where was I?"

"You had just covered the benefits of induction. But I am wondering how your philosophy addresses the challenge of Callicles, that individuals can just redefine the concept of virtue in accordance with their self interest."

"That is the proper question. Let me first note that philosophers in our tradition had sought answers to two questions for generations: what is the ultimate nature of reality, and how can that ultimate reality be reconciled with the changes we see happening around us all the time. Without proper science, an array of competing theories emerged with no good way to make an intelligent choice."

He continued. "Socrates turned away from questions of metaphysics to focus on ethics, thinking our experience as social animals would provide enough of an anchor for common concepts like virtue. Callicles' argument for virtue as self interest, however unsatisfying it may seem, does make the case that we need to ground the concept of virtue in something deeper than experience if we are to show that virtue is something more than a matter of personal preference. Plato's theories of an ultimate reality beyond experience is an admirable answer to Callicles, but not without issues of its own."

"My model holds that all things consist of matter and form. Matter is the physical stuff of which we are made. Form is like a potential energy or guiding force that is specific to every type of living thing.

Form determines the shape of the matter of a thing as it progresses through the normal life cycle for the kind of thing it is. For an oak tree, for instance, form determines that its initial state is the humble acorn. But under the right conditions, its form will drive it to sprout into a sapling, and eventually grow into a fully mature tree, with leaves of a certain kind, and bark of a certain kind, and the ability to produce its own acorns."

"How does that answer the challenge of Callicles?"

"Well, the form of a human as a social animal drives a person to mature in certain ways, just like the oak tree. And the very definition of a social animal is an animal that relies on the behavior of other social animals, and that, in turn, behaves in ways that meet certain minimal social expectations. That is the nature of social animals."

"Just as we find that some oak trees do not grow to the full potential of their form, some social animals also do not grow to the full potential of their form. The fact that some acorns don't fulfill their potential as oak trees doesn't change the nature of an oak tree. The fact that some social animals do not mature into their full arete, or virtue, as a social animal does not change the nature of social animals."

"Ah, I see."

"An interesting and elegant perspective, Aristotle. But it still seems to me that Callicles could argue that his idea of virtue is the true virtue of a social animal, based on the inherent order of the strong dominating the weak."

"A sound point, Plato. There are certainly counterexamples Callicles could use to support such a claim. But my argument is inductive. In this case, it does not require the absence of counterexamples, only that the weight of evidence supports my hypothesis over that of Callicles. And I rely upon the 158 constitutions of the Greek city-states to support my claim."

"Of course, Callicles could then argue these city-states represent an exception in the history of all human societies around the world. I don't believe he has the evidence to support that view, however."

A large golden eagle soared gracefully in front of where the three were walking, braking with its impressively large wings before coming to rest on the stump of a dead tree.

"Einstein!," Plato exclaimed. "Perhaps you can weigh in on whose theory you favor, mine or this upstart student of mine."

"Certainly, Plato. First of all, your notion that there is an immutable element to reality is correct for the universe as we experience it. And you are correct to seek this ultimate and unchanging aspect of reality in the realm of ideas. A good part of my own work was proving that individual frames of reference are relative to the observer, and discovering some ultimate ideas that describe reality, like my equation $E = mc2$."

Plato pulled back his lips to show his teeth in the silliest example of a dog smiling that I have ever seen. "That is good to hear," he said.

"But not all reality is in the realm of ideas," Einstein continued, "and the true power of a theory lies in its ability to describe and predict what we will observe in the physical world."

"Aristotle's model of the union of potential energy and matter is compelling. In my day, biologists unlocked chemical blueprints that served the purpose of guiding the growth of individuals within each species. And the equation I cited earlier is all about how energy shapes matter, and the relationship between the two."

"But really, the point I want to leave you all with is this: a theory is not only important for what it describes, but also for the areas it identifies where your knowledge can't quite reach. Good theories fire our imagination, drive us to ask the next question, and to build the tools to answer that question. There was a great deal that was beyond your ability to see, but your pursuit of the truth ultimately led from a society with no science to a society that provided a foundation for the modern scientific method. For every generation of scientists, there are things that are unknown and unknowable until some advance allows us to extend our intellectual reach."

"Look, I appreciate being able to listen to you all," I said, "but I am no further along in knowing how I got here, or how I am going to answer questions in court, than I was when we started. It seems that, in spite of all the great theories, we still have difficulty getting to a point where we can say we know something."

"That is as good a reason to go spend some time with Descartes as I have ever heard. You did say that is where you are going next, right?"

Plato nodded.

The eagle continued. "Descartes has a way of breaking things down to the basics. Once you talk to him a bit, I think you will realize that you know more than you think you do. Thank you for letting an old eagle join in your conversation!"

"Thank you!," they chorused. With a thrust from its perch and a few powerful strokes, Einstein was quickly circling far above them.

"Aristotle, thank you for your time," I said.

"Oh, it was my pleasure," he replied. "Good luck to you!"

"Plato, it is always wonderful to discuss and debate with you. Thank you. Now I suppose its time for me to leave you both. There is a patch of clover over there that looks lovely. See you again, I hope!" The big stallion turned and trotted to where the clover grew thick in the shadow of the trees on the far side of the meadow.

"Back up the hill for us, I'm afraid," Plato said. "But I know a short-cut from here. Follow me."

Given the length of time they had spent walking with Aristotle, the trip back to the top of the hill was surprisingly fast. When they got there, they found Descartes and Socrates deep in conversation, a concerned look on both their faces.

The Foxes Challenge Knowledge and Truth

"I knew you should not have talked with the foxes. Nothing good ever comes of it. What have they done to put those frowns on your faces?," Plato said as they drew close to the retriever and the raccoon.

"Oh, come now," Socrates said, ignoring Plato and looking directly at me. "First things first—how did your visits with Plato and Aristotle go?"

"They were quite amazing. Both shared powerful models. Frankly, it's all a bit overwhelming. And Einstein the Eagle joined us for a few minutes as well, which was pretty incredible. But, truthfully, I am still pretty confused about how I can know which model I should believe, and which is true, and how any of this can help me get home."

"Well, that's a great connection to what Descartes and I did as well," Socrates replied. "We've both been noticing a great increase in people who feel the same way you do—overwhelmed. Let's face it, the volume of information that washes over us every day is pretty intense. People react differently to that—parents, for instance, struggle to balance taking care of their families with keeping up with what is happening in their jobs and in the world around them. A lot of people are looking for ways to simplify the volume of information with which they have to deal."

"The foxes have started a network that we feel takes advantage of people who are overwhelmed. They tell stories that either misrepresent the facts or create a false impression of the truth by carefully omitting key facts. The fox network's very biased information plays up overly simplistic explanations of everything you can imagine. Religion and patriotism are two big models the fox network is using to make money by selling simplicity."

"Religious beliefs are usually something people receive from their parents, and are therefore never truly examined with a critical eye, at least not publicly. In this country, the prevailing view is that we are a Christian nation. People who argue for the rights of non-Christians under the banner of religious freedom or civil liberties, along with people who argue for an individual woman's right to choose whether or not to have a baby, are portrayed as the enemy, even though they are arguing for rights protected by the Constitution. These civil liberties arguments are mostly advanced by Democrats, so many Christians become Republicans by default."

Socrates continued, "Ironically, the same Republicans who resist arguments for civil liberties in matters like religious freedom for non-Christians and abortion will be the first to protest that their civil liberties are violated by laws requiring background checks for the purchase of guns, or restricting gatherings to protect the vulnerable from the virus."

"It is as if they are incapable of recognizing that that the right to religious freedom is as much a constitutional right as the right to bear arms. Or that there is a contradiction in arguing that terminating an embryo or fetus before it can survive outside the womb is "murder," but not wearing a mask is your right even though it will enable the spread of a virus that will kill more fully alive, but vulnerable Americans."

"On the patriotism front, people tend to support our government against all other governments under the assumption that America is always right. For Christians, our government is supposed to give us the freedom that is consistent with God's law. That means "patriotic" Americans—and Christians in particular—support President Dumb. After all, he is a Republican. So we attack people who point out where he has lied or misstated the facts, because they are mostly Democrats. We support draining the swamp, whatever that means, and building a wall that we are sure will stop illegal immigration from the south. But we overlook the fact that there have been more corruption scandals in President Dumb's administration than in the previous administration."

"We forget, or never realized, that it was Republicans who opposed doubling the size of the border patrol and creating a national strategy for barriers and security on the southern border in 2013. Republicans opposed immigration reform and border security laws in 2013 because they didn't want to give a Democratic president a win on immigration. But the network of foxes has successfully spun the facts and convinced Americans that Democrats are corrupt and unpatriotic, and that Republicans are the only ones who want a secure southern border."

Descartes nodded vigorously. "The foxes use simplified models to create artificial alignments between ideas to which people are emotionally attached and other movements or personalities that can pay for the influence. They use these alignments to filter out unwanted truth, not just noise."

"People really lose their ability to tell true from false. Many people are vulnerable and can be pushed into supporting whatever cause the foxes and their allies want to support. Socrates and I were just talking about how we might fight against this problem."

"Did you come up with any ideas?," Plato asked.

"Yes, we did," Socrates replied. "It's really based on Descartes' model, so I'll let him explain."

Descartes

Excited to have a chance to speak, the raccoon began, "Many years ago, when I was confronting the dilemma of how to determine what I could truly believe, I realized that almost all of the things I thought I knew rested on an entire network of related ideas, some of which were less reliable than others. I hit upon the idea of discarding any idea of which I was not certain, until I was left with the core of what I 'knew'."

He paused and took a sip of water from a pool that had gathered in a nearby tree trunk, and then, turning back to them, he continued. "I realized that the only thing I could be absolutely certain of was the fact that I was having these thoughts. The content of the thoughts might be an illusion or a distortion, as our friend Plato so elegantly points out in his Allegory of the Cave. But because of what a thought is, the implication of my having thoughts—regardless of the content—is that there is an 'I.' There has to be an entity having thoughts if I am, in fact, thinking. As I told my friends at the time, "I think, therefore I am."

"This may seem like a trivial point, but it is a critical first step for two reasons. First, it is a powerful rebuttal to skeptics who say we cannot know anything, even if all we can prove is that we exist. Second, it immediately confronts us with the essential second step each of us must ask ourselves: who or what is this 'I' that exists?"

"I see!," I blurted, unable to contain my excitement. "And that is precisely the question that Socrates, Plato and Aristotle answer with their assertions that we are social animals, although each with slightly different justifications."

"Right! Consider three points on the spectrum of how we proceed from the point of acknowledging our existence, as creatures confronted with the world of experience. Rejecting the validity of all of our sense data leads to a complete inability to function effectively, or at least, to a kind of nihlilism that is hardly satisfying. Acknowledging that our sense data has flaws leads us to adopt strategies to mitigate the flaws, like co-operating with other creatures with whom we can communicate. Here is where our friends' theories fit in the spectrum. Or we can assume that our sense data is 100 percent accurate, and attempt to navigate our lives on that basis."

"Assuming that our sense data is 100 percent accurate will soon bring us into conflict with others whose perceptions are different from our own. That seems to be where your President Dumb is. How we choose—as individuals—to answer the question of who and what we are determines so much about our character. And each of us must answer that question for ourselves—no one can do it for us."

"I Kant, I Kant," Plato interrupted excitedly, suddenly leaping to his feet and running around with great energy.

"Of course you can," Descartes responded.

"No!" the black puppy exclaimed, "Immanuel Kant is coming!" The dog darted away from the group in the direction of the spot where we first crested the hill. A medium-sized black bear lumbered toward them.

The Bear Imperative

"Hello there, Immanuel!," Socrates cried out.

"Hi, Socrates," the bear responded. "Are you throwing a party with-out me?"

"Just an unplanned gathering of friends, to which you are always invited. My friend Stephen was just getting up to speed on some of our models." Turning to me, he added, "Stephen, meet Immanuel Kant."

"It's a pleasure to meet you, sir," I said. "With the help of this group, I have just made a connection between Descarte's cogito and the systems of Socrates, Plato and Aristotle—something that eluded me in 16 years of schooling. It's quite exhilarating!"

"Excellent! And what would you say if I asked you to describe the most striking feature shared by the philosophies of these four great thinkers?"

I thought for a moment before responding. "I suppose that each of them, in their own way, emphasized what we do not know or cannot know."

"Well said. And there is great wisdom in the practice of humility when considering the standard of knowledge. None of these philosophers are skeptics, though—they all believe we can know things—but each chose to emphasize the limits of knowledge as they experienced those limits, even as they try to teach us how best to gain knowledge. Socrates and Plato recognized the limits of our sensory experience, but seem to think we can transcend those limits through the perfection of reason. Aristotle uses experience to move away from such a strong emphasis on perfecting reason, exalting instead the achievement of the virtue of a social animal—a proper balance between reason and emotion. Descartes echoes the limitations of sense and the power of reason in his famous proof that we know we exist. My own model has much in common with all four of these towering intellects; but there is one point of difference that I would like to call to your attention—can you guess what it might be?"

For the first time since waking up with Socrates staring at me, I was conscious of being hungry. Really hungry. Hungry enough to eat a bear, in fact. But wise enough to fight through my pangs of hunger, with a supreme act of will, to focus on the question Kant had asked. The old bear was looking at me quizzically.

Deep within me, from the dark maw of my empty stomach, realizing that the path to food went directly through being able to answer the question, I found enough energy to exclaim "Precognitive!" with the force of projectile vomiting. "The others outlined ways we could perfect or balance by improving ourselves through acts of will, but you identified limits that were precognitive, and therefore could never be overcome."

"That is correct! My forms of intuition were effectively given to us as the mechanisms for perceiving the world of experience. We have no choice but to absorb the shared world of experience through minds that are limited to perceiving events as ordered in time and ordered in space. And we have no way of knowing if the events we are experiencing actually do have the characteristics of time and space, or if reality beyond our sensory experience is somehow exempt from the laws of time and space as we know them."

"There is a further point I want you to remember: Socrates, Plato, Aristotle and I agree that we are social animals, although I do not emphasize it nearly as much as my Greek friends. For Socrates and Plato, the perfection of reason had to be a social endeavor. Aristotle emphasized our social nature more as a function of the fundamental form of the human animal. In my case, once you accept that we all share the common limits of my forms of intuition, then you are left with only one possible rule to guide our conduct. We are bound to see things from different perspectives because of our precognitive limits; therefore, the proper ethical rule should consider the perspectives of others to be as valid as our own. Given that, we must act only in ways that we could will as a universal rule for all others—that is essentially what I call the Categorical Imperative."

"Wow! I never thought of it in that way." I could not be sure if I was experiencing yet another wave of epiphany, or if I was about to faint from hunger. "I don't mean to be rude, but I am starving! Is there any place I can get some food?"

Socrates got a pained expression on his face, "Of course! It is late, and you haven't eaten since…"

"Yesterday, I guess," I finished. "If only we were in season for the fruit, I could snack on apples and cherries."

"Right. But for now, that doesn't do us any good," Plato said thoughtfully. "The food bank is probably our best bet. I think they are actually preparing meals in a shelter near there."

"Good thinking! I'm afraid I won't be welcome there, though, so I will say my goodbyes for now," Kant rumbled. "Just remember, when you disagree with someone, consider whether the disagreement, or the root of the disagreement, is precognitive. If it is, the disagreement is not a matter of choice, and the only true solution is for both sides to realize that."

"Thank you!" I exclaimed. For the third or fourth time since waking up in front of Socrates, a feeling of profound enlightenment swept over me.

"And do come back in the fall when the fruit is out. We can dine together. You can even bring one of Donny Dumb's Republicans... I will need some extra calories to get ready for hibernation," the bear chuckled. "Just kidding, of course." The bear and racoon turned and rambled off together.

"See you later, Stephen," Descartes called over his shoulder.

"Come, Plato, let's get to the food bank," Socrates remarked. "It's not far, Stephen. Hang in there."

CHAPTER 2

Jesus, the Shelter and the Attorney Gerbil

It turned out that the woods through which Socrates and I had me-andered on the way to the Model-makers' Workshop wrapped around the southwestern corner of the town. Plato led the way back towards the pond, then took a fork off to the right and up a hill, heading generally east.

The trio emerged from the woods at the head of a cul-de-sac, with a series of buildings that looked like warehouses flanking the road leading southeast away from the circle of pavement they were crossing. A small cluster of people stood near the doorway of the second building on the right. A sign over the door read "Green Valley Shelter & Food Bank."

As the three drew near, a black man wearing a cloth mask emerged from the doorway. "Is there anyone here for the shelter, or are you all here for the food bank?" the man asked cheerfully.

The group in front of them indicated they were there for the food bank. At the urging of Socrates, I told the man that I was there for the shelter.

"Okay, everyone take a mask from this basket, and put it on before you come inside." He motioned to a basket of bluish disposable masks hanging next to the door. "Then follow me." He led the way into the entrance of the food bank. He motioned to some chairs scattered in front of a low counter as he raised a section of the counter and retreated into the back. "Wait here, please."

After a few minutes, he emerged from the back room, pushing a cart on which rested four cardboard containers.

"If you are here for the food bank, please come on up." He distributed one carton of food to each of the four people who approached, ensuring each signed a roster acknowledging receipt of the food before they departed, leaving just me and the two dogs sitting in the lobby of the food bank.

"Shelter?" he asked.

"Yes," I replied.

"Me, too," he said, crossing the small lobby and securing the door from the inside.

Then, leading the way behind the counter, he said, "Follow me."

I did as he said, and the dogs padded along behind me, as if this was a familiar routine. They passed through a doorway and into the storeroom for the food bank. The shelves were almost entirely bare. The food bank man turned and stuck his elbow out to tap with mine in a virus-safe greeting, "I'm Jesus."

"I'm Stephen," I said. Indicating my companions, I added, "Socrates and Plato."

"I've seen these two before," he said, kneeling and giving each a scratch on the head and affectionate pat on the shoulders. The dogs each craned their necks, as if trying to position their heads so the scratch hit just the right place.

"Will you help me serve dinner for the shelter side?" he asked.

"Sure," I said, wondering how we could feed anyone with the shelves as empty as they seemed. As if on cue, a heavy-set, red-faced man bustled towards them from the other side of the storeroom.

"You gave away all the food!" he screamed. "How are we going to feed the shelter? There are 113 people staying with us tonight!"

"114," Jesus answered calmly. "Don't worry, there's enough. I'll take care of the shelter."

"What do you mean, there's enough? There's no where near enough! All I see are a couple of cans of sardines and some boxes of crackers. You were supposed to leave the food I had placed on these yellow shelves for the shelter meal! You gave it all away! What do you expect me to do for tomorrow morning?"

"Don't worry about the shelter meal tonight, there's enough. Trust me. Did you call the food factory and the grocery stores to let them know we are out of food and need more? You have to do that. Let me worry about feeding the shelter."

"I called yesterday. They gave us what they had. I can't call back again today! We were supposed to make that last!"

"We were supposed to make it last?" Jesus said. "How do we do that when there are hungry people who need food? You have to call them back and tell them we need more. It is not your responsibility if they say no. But it is your responsibility to make sure everyone knows what we need. Come on, let's call them together."

They all followed red-faced man to a small office near a door on the far side of the storeroom. He sat at his desk and reluctantly dialed the phone, hitting the speaker button as he did so they could all hear.

"Greenhouse Gas Food Factory," a gruff voice crackled on the other end of the phone line.

"Jim, this is Bob at The Green Valley shelter..."

"Bob, we just gave you food last night. We don't have any more to give you. We've got shareholders, you know, and they deserve a return on their investment."

"Okay, Jim, I suppose they do, but the people here need to eat. There are a lot of hungry people these days, and I don't have any control over how many show up. We need your help."

"Well, we all got problems. I just got told I have jury duty in a few days. And I am telling you, I cannot help with more food. Not now. Not again. Not so soon. Goodbye, Bob." They all heard the phone click on the speaker, and the line went dead.

Red-faced man made six more calls, three to the grocery stores, two to restaurants, and one to another food factory in an adjacent town.

Each call met with similar results. No one was interested in giving more food away.

"I told you. No one can help. We were supposed to make that food last. What are we going to do?"

"Don't worry, Bob. Let me feed the shelter. There's enough. But you need to keep calling people every day to let them know our situation. And tomorrow you should add in the mayor's office and the sheriff's office. They can help. Now go home."

Bob left, leaving Jesus and me and the two dogs alone in the storeroom adjacent to the shelter dining room.

"Okay, Stephen, let's make dinner happen. You run the serving line, taking the plates from me through this window and handing them to the guests as they come through the line."

"If you say so, but I don't see how we are going to feed more than a few people with this," I said, motioning to the small pile of cans of fish and boxes of crackers. As I headed toward the doorway leading to the serving area, I saw Jesus saying a blessing over the food. It wasn't long before hungry guests started to line up for the shelter's evening meal.

What happened next left me completely astonished. Jesus started handing plates through the window, but each plate contained a good portion of hot baked fish, macaroni and cheese, steamed broccoli, and even a small piece of iced sheet cake. The hungry guests accepted the plates gratefully, helping themselves to juice or water from the drink machines before settling into plastic chairs to enjoy their meal. When the last guest had been served, Jesus passed plates through for the two of us and for the dogs as well.

By this time I was very hungry, and went to work first on the mound of mac and cheese. Eventually, when I had eaten enough to soothe my hunger pangs a bit, I turned to Jesus and blurted out, "That was incredible! How did you do that?"

"Oh," Jesus chuckled, " I guess you could say my father taught me to cook."

"Yeah, but there wasn't anywhere near enough food to feed everyone. Where did you get the macaroni and broccoli? And the cake?"

"All the food that was there was given. There is a lot of power in gifts, for both giver and receiver. Often you have to humble yourself to ask for help, and that is hard for many. But there is a lot of power in humility, too. So the short answer to your question is, I just asked for help."

A million thoughts and questions tumbled over one another in my head, but Jesus' cell phone rang before I could ask the next question.

"Green Valley Shelter," he said, hitting the speaker button and laying the phone on the table so I could listen.

A soft voice crackled up from the phone. "Hey, I got a donation, but I need help unloading the truck. It's a lot. I'm out by the delivery doors to your warehouse."

"Awesome! We'll be right out!"

The Good Thief

Jesus flipped on the warehouse lights, and they strode down the aisles of empty rack toward the dock door, the two dogs still padding along behind. He hit a green button mounted alongside a metal rail to activate the opening mechanism, and a low hum testified to the unseen machinery raising the door before them.

Outside, a deep twilight swallowed the pale circles of light that emanated from the roof of the warehouse to the expanse of pavement below. They could make out the hulking shadow of a tractor-trailer in the darkness beyond, hunched around taillights that gleamed like the two red eyes of a sinister box thingy.

The door to the cab opened. A figure climbed down and came towards them. As the driver stepped into the yellow light, they could make out a young, wiry woman with shoulder-length brown hair.

"If you guys can ground guide, I'll back up to the door."

I grabbed two flashlights with red cone filter attachments from a wall-mounted basket by the door, handed one to Jesus, and followed him outside and down a short flight of stairs. The driver swung back up in the cab of the truck, then pulled it forward and away from the warehouse. With Jesus and I waving flashlights on either side of the dock door, she carefully backed the semi up until it was flush with the bumpers on the dock door.

"Thank you for this," Jesus told her as the three headed back for the stairs. "You are just in time—we just served the last meal we could have served without this donation."

"Well, we are glad to help," the woman answered.

"I thought you guys weren't able to give anything tonight—what changed?," Jesus asked.

"I guess my boss must have changed his mind. I just take stuff where I'm told to."

"Well, thank you. By the way, my name is Jesus, and this is Stephen."

"Oh, I'm Robin."

Jesus brought a forklift up while Robin raised the back of her truck. Over the next forty-five minutes, he offloaded twenty-three pallets of food. When he was done, he gave her a receipt.

Robin pulled down the door to the truck after the last pallet was removed.

"Thank you, again, for all this. You and your boss should come back to the shelter some time and see all the people you have helped. We can hang out," Jesus told her.

"We will do that," Robin said. "You guys have a good night." She left through the back door, and I secured it behind her. It took her just another minute or two to get back behind the wheel, and the truck pulled slowly away from the dock door.

Jesus reached over to hit the button and close the warehouse dock door, but froze when he saw the light of a cell phone in the grass across the pavement. "I wonder who that is?" he said.

"Let's go find out," I said, unlocking the back door again. We went down the stairs and headed toward the strip of grass that separated the asphalt of the warehouse parking and loading area from the street.

A Neighbor in Need

As we neared the edge of the pavement, the blue light of the cell phone disappeared, and a hasty rustling indicated whoever was there was trying to leave in a hurry.

"We're not here to hurt you," Jesus said, "It's okay. You don't have to run away. We won't come any closer. We just wanted to invite you to come inside the shelter. There's a shelter in this building behind me. We have room, and you are welcome."

A small voice answered in an unsteady tone, "I don't want any trouble. I can't pay anything."

"It's okay. You don't have to pay anything. My name is Jesus, and this is Stephen. I work at the shelter. Why don't you come inside? Have you heard of The Green Valley Shelter? It's a safe place."

"I guess that would be okay," the small voice said. "I don't have any money or anything," the voice added as if still worried the two might try to rob her.

"How about if I walk out in front of you and lead you to the front door of the shelter. There are nice people there who can check you in. When was your last meal? We can get you something to eat inside, also." Then, to me, Jesus added, "Stephen, can you please make sure the back door of the warehouse is locked? I will meet you back in the dining area, once I get..." Turning back to the small voice, "What's your name?"

"I'm Jane," the small voice answered.

"...once I get Jane checked in to the shelter."

"Sure," I said, "I'll go take care of the back door."

As I retreated across the asphalt, I heard the small voice volunteer, "I had a sandwich this afternoon, but I am hungry."

"Okay, you just walk behind me and I will lead you to the entrance. Once you're checked in, we'll get you something to eat." I saw Jesus start to walk, leading the young woman towards the front of the shelter.

The dogs and I climbed the stairs to the rear of the warehouse. Once inside, I secured the door behind me, hit the red button to close the dock door, and headed across the storeroom toward the dining area.

No sooner had I settled into a plastic chair than Jesus emerged from the doorway leading to the front of the shelter.

"Staff will bring Jane back for a meal once they get her checked in," he said. "You wait here for her, and I'll get some food ready." He strode behind the counter and through the doorway to the kitchen area. After a few minutes of rustling, a loud chime from the microwave testified that food was on the way.

A staff member entered the dining area from a door at the far end that I had not noticed before. I assumed the young woman with her was Jane. She looked pale, no more than seventeen, with medium brown hair. I rose to greet them. After brief introductions, the staff member retreated through the door from which she had come, leaving Jane and I standing near the table as Jesus emerged from the kitchen with a plate that looked like the same meal he had served earlier in the evening.

"Get yourself some water or juice," he said, motioning to the machine against the wall. He set the plate down on the table and sat down next to me and the dogs. Jane returned with her drink and sat down in front of the plate of food.

"Thank you," she said, before turning her attention to the food.

"Glad to help. That's what we are here for." Turning to me, he added "I could use your help again with the breakfast meal, if you can do that."

"Sure," I said.

Jane ate quietly. Jesus continued speaking to me, allowing her to enjoy her meal. "It will be time to start preparing breakfast before you know it. If you can plan your morning to meet me here a few minutes before 7, that will be perfect."

"That's easy," I said. I suddenly realized I had no cell phone or watch to set an alarm.

"Will there be an alarm clock or something near where I sleep?"

"We'll figure that out when we get you settled."

Jane finished the last of her cake, and Jesus turned back to her. "It's late, but perhaps tomorrow we can chat a bit to see how else we can help."

"Okay," she said, adding nervously, "I have a follow-up appointment at the Planned Parenthood clinic at 11."

Jesus nodded. "That isn't too far from here, but we can probably get you a ride in the morning. Let's get everyone settled in for the night."

The trio stood and walked through the doorway at the far end of the dining area, emerging in the lobby. Jane headed to her assigned dorm, and Jesus led me to the desk to get me checked in. Before saying good night, he made sure I was given an alarm clock and flashlight along with some basic linen and toiletries.

The lights were out in my assigned space, but I managed to make myself comfortable with the help of the flashlight. I set the alarm for six o'clock, and was asleep as soon as my head hit the pillow.

The Attorney Gerbil

I was back in my dream again.

Whatever had hit the window had knocked me off the ledge and into the air. I thought it must have been a bird, aiming to make me lunch, but the bulletproof glass had done its work and I fluttered down to the rug unharmed. Everyone was leaving the Oval Office in any event, so I launched myself into the air, alternating between gaining altitude and gliding until I regained my original perch on the brown wood frame. I folded my wings and settled in to rest until the arrival of the Attorney Gerbil.

Time passed. A disturbance in the air accompanied the opening of the door and the re-entry of the President and his Chief of Staff. No sooner had they reached the big wooden desk then the intercom crackled and a voice crackled, "Sir, the Attorney Gerbil is here."

Great, send him in."

The Honorable DamLow Bar entered the Oval Office from a different door that that used by Dumb and Pasturepie a moment before.

"Hello, DamLow. We have something very important that requires your attention. But first, you know, I have been meaning to ask you about your name—it's quite unique—I don't think I've ever met another DamLow. Is it a family thing?"

"Kind of. My father's name was just Low Bar. But he always wanted more for me."

"Well, that's the American dream, right?"

"DamRight."

The president nodded. "Well, down to business. I want to issue an executive order making myself king, and people keep telling me there's a problem with the Constitution or the law or something, and I need you to fix it."

"Of course, Mr. President."

"Wait, you can do that?" Paul Pasturepie queried. "Don't get me wrong, I think it's awesome, but I'm interested in the 'how' of it, so I can support."

"Well, I mean, the Constitution is our master law," Bar replied. "And the president is the executive charged with implementing that law. There's some problematic verbiage, and people will raise a fuss about checks and balances and such, but it's nothing we can't plow through and paper over, if that's what the president wants. I mean, there IS a precedent."

"There is? You mean King George?" Pasturepie asked, a surprised look on his face.

"Well, yes and no. We ARE still talking about the Constitution, which means we probably need a precedent after 1787, so King George is kind of out of the question. But the Reichstag Fire Decree and the Enabling Act, now, I think we can work with those."

President Dumb nodded approvingly.

"And Mr. President, to Paul's point, it certainly wouldn't hurt if you could get the fox network to start laying the foundation for making 'being a Tory' cool again."

"Of course. Now let's think about timing. Paul, what do you think?"

The intercom crackled again before the Chief of Staff could speak. "Mr. President, Secretary Pompidou called to speak with you. I told him you were in a meeting. He said to remind you the Israeli Prime

Minister's birthday is coming up? And he would like to come get some face time with you."

"My god," the president muttered. He pressed the button to reply, "Thank you, send the Prime Minister one of those Barry and Goliath hams, and send one to the Israeli embassy in honor of his birthday as well. With my compliments. And tell Pompidou I said thank you and that he'll make a fine president someday."

"Yes, sir."

"What a tool!" The president muttered almost under his breath.

Paul Pasturepie spoke, "Sir, the Israeli Prime Minister is Jewish..."

"I know that! And I don't care. No one really follows those kinds of rules, except for show. People will take anything, especially if it's from me and it's in the right packaging."

"If you say so, sir. With regard to the timing of this king stuff, I wanted to remind you there is the rally in Green Valley in a couple days, Mr. President. Maybe we should meet after that to discuss your kingship further."

"Oh, that's right! I'm looking forward to that trip. A meeting post-rally to discuss timing sounds good to me. DamLow, what are your thoughts?"

"I will think about timing and will be prepared for a post-rally meeting. Off the top of my head, though, in line with the recent Fourth of July holiday, we might want to synchronize messaging with something like, 'Without King George, There is No Declaration of Independence,' or something like that."

The president smiled with perverse pleasure. "DamLow Bar, you're my man! It feels SO good to finally have an Attorney Gerbil that knows how to do his job!"

I was horrified at what I had just heard. One of my legs slipped off the wood ledge where I was perched. In the glass, I could see my torso growing rapidly. Soon I would fall off the frame completely, and would certainly become visible to the men below. I had to get out of the Oval Office before I was discovered!

I launched into the air, expecting the light flutter I had experienced before. Instead, I felt the sickening pull of gravity and plunged toward the floor. I fluttered furiously, but my wings were no match for my bloated body, now the size of a small bird. Madly trying to slow my descent, I careened into a blue antique vase and landed on a narrow table with a thud. The vase tipped, fell, and shattered on the floor with a loud crash that went on and on and on...

CHAPTER 3

Clinic, University and Gladimeer's Embassy

All I could think of was finding a way to stop the loud noise. I practically jumped out of bed, feeling quickly for the alarm clock and turning it off. I fell back into a seated position on the bed, holding my head with both hands. Remembering the shelter, and Jesus, and all that had happened in the past 24 hours, I got up and started to head for the bathroom.

Realizing that Socrates and Plato had risen silently and were following me, I made a quick detour to let them outside. Both found places to pee and then joined me in the doorway. I left both dogs in the dining room and headed back to the bathrooom to shower, shave and get dressed.

Finished, I returned to the dining area to find Jesus happily preparing a simple meal of scrambled eggs, sausage, cereal, toast and berries. This time there was no mystery where the food came from. I took up my post out front, passing plates to hungry guests as they came through the line. Eventually, when everyone had been fed and the dogs were happily devouring plates of scraps, Jesus and I sat with Jane and ate our breakfast.

"I have to take the shelter van to the hospital to check on some former guests," Jesus said, between bites. "I can drop you at the clinic on my way. Stephen, you should come and walk with Jane into the clinic. Sometimes there are protesters trying to block the entrance."

"Thank you," Jane replied. "My parents kicked me out of the house when they found out I was getting an abortion. The people at our church turned me away too. They said I was going against God's law and I would be punished. I didn't think you would help me."

"Is your family Christian?" Jesus asked.

"Yes. They are very religious."

"They may be religious, but they do not understand the teachings of Jesus. Look, I am not going to pretend I am okay with your decision to have an abortion. I am not. But I would never let that disagreement interfere with my duty to love you. Do you remember what Jesus said when they asked him to identify the most important of all the commandments?"

"Yes. Love the Lord with all your heart. And then he said there was another commandment like that in importance—love your neighbor as yourself."

"I'm impressed. Very nice. Do you remember what happened next?"

"They asked Jesus who they should consider their neighbor, and Jesus responded with the parable of the good Samaritan."

"Wow. You know your stuff. You must have spent some time reading your scriptures. How did you ever have time to get knocked up?"

Jane smiled for the first time since they found her outside and let out a little chuckle. "That's not a very Jesus-like thing to say." She was smiling down at her hands, folded in front of her on the table, obviously relieved to be in a conversation with people who weren't mad at her.

"Well, I am glad it made you laugh. The thing people forget about the parable is that the Samaritans and Jews hated each other—like Democrats and Republicans. So the real lesson there is that the people you are called to love like yourself are precisely the ones you are most challenged to love—the ones who think differently and look differently and act differently than you. We aren't built to all be the same or to agree with each other all the time."

"Thank you for that."

Socrates raised his head and spoke from his spot on the floor. "Jesus' Good Samaritan story is a beautiful expression of the moral duty we have as social animals."

"Wait, you mean you can read, too?" I asked in surprise.

"Of course," Socrates said. Then he added, "Well, I do need help turning the pages."

Jesus laughed, "Well, we all need help with something, Socrates." Then, to Jane, he continued. "The other thing that I wish so-called Christians would remember is what Jesus did not say. He did not say 'Thou shalt not kill' was the most important commandment, or thou shalt not covet thy neighbor's goods." Jesus glanced at me as he said this, then continued. "And do you remember what Jesus said when they brought him the woman who had been caught in adultery?"

"Yeah, they wanted to stone her, and he said the one who is perfect should throw the first stone, or something like that."

"Right, and when he and the woman were left alone, he asked her if there was no one left to condemn her, and she said there was no one left. Do you remember what Jesus said after that?"

"Neither do I condemn you."

"Right again." Jesus looked up from his own hands, and saw tears streaming down Jane's face.

I grabbed some napkins and passed them to her across the table. She took them and dried her face.

Jesus said, "I didn't mean to upset you, but those are the most important passages in the scriptures. Anybody who isn't struggling to live those scriptures every day isn't living a Christian life. They may be very religious, but they aren't following Jesus.

You have been placed in my path, and my job as Jesus—as a Christian—is to be the good Samaritan for you. To expand the range of healthy choices available to you, perhaps. Not to be your judge, jury and executioner. Not to agree with every decision you make. Not to change your mind in every case. I am sorry that your parents and your church couldn't see that."

"We should get you over to the clinic," Jesus said. "You might want to get something else to drink before we leave."

"Yes," Jane said, heading over to fill her glass at the machine.

"That was really powerful," I said to Jesus while she was gone.

"Thanks. Drives me nuts that people use religion for all the wrong reasons and forget the most important stuff. When you walk her into the clinic, make sure they are going to counsel her on all options, including having the baby and putting it up for adoption. And make sure she knows she can stay at the shelter as long as she needs to."

Jane returned, and quickly downed her water. The three walked over and put their trays on a window like the one where Stephen had gotten the plates from Jesus at the beginning of the meal. A couple of shelter residents were cleaning the dishes on the other side of the window. They headed across the dining room toward the front lobby area. Socrates and Plato, who had curled up on the floor near the table after finishing their food, rose and padded along behind them.

As they walked across the lobby, Jesus veered toward the front entrance. "You two need to sign out," he said. "Make sure they know you are coming back tonight. I'll get the van and meet you out front."

When they emerged from the front door of the shelter, Jane and Stephen found a white shuttle van, engine running, sitting outside. A logo with the words "Green Valley Shelter ~ The Path Home" in green letters was emblazoned on the side of the van. Stephen and Jane climbed into the sliding side door, and the two dogs jumped in behind them. Stephen pulled it closed behind him, and buckled himself into the bench seat next to Jane, who sat directly behind Jesus.

Jesus handed each of them a fresh mask, then put one on himself. He moved the gear shift from "Park" to "Drive" and the vehicle started to move. They turned right out of the parking lot, then left at the next stop sign, and straight on northward, following what looked to be a fairly major street.

Clinic

Protesters were indeed present—marching, chanting, and blocking access—when the van pulled up across the street from the clinic.

"Do you want me to call the police?" I asked.

"No, please don't do that. As a black man, I am more likely to be arrested and killed than any of these white protesters, regardless of whether my behavior violates any law. Let me try to talk to them first."

We got out of the van, leaving windows cracked for the dogs. I poured some water in a dish for them as well, and slid the door closed. Turning, our little group headed toward the entrance to the clinic together. Seeing us, the handful of protesters clustered around the entrance, blocking access and chanting, "It's a child, not a choice! It's a child, not a choice!" People in the crowd held signs with slogans like "Sinner Repent!", "Life is Sacred!", and "Let God Plan Parenthood!".

Jesus stopped in front of the protesters blocking the door, and addressed the person who seemed to be the leader. "What are you doing?"

"Saving lives!" the man replied. Others cheered.

"But it is legal for the clinic to be here. And it is legal for us to go into the clinic. What you are doing is not legal. Are you trying to break the law?"

"We want to change the law! God's law says murdering the unborn is evil! When President Dumb appoints more conservative judges, they will change the laws of the United States so they are the same as God's law!" More cheers.

"You know, they passed a law in 1920 making alcohol illegal. Did that law stop people from drinking?"

"No."

"How about all the laws that launched the war on drugs? How did that turn out? Did it stop illegal drug use?"

"No."

"So you are supporting a president because you think he might appoint judges that will change a law, even though you know that changing the law won't change the behavior that you are trying to change. Is that right?"

"Making abortion illegal will at least make our country's law support God's law!" Some cheers, but not as many as before.

"You are Christians, right?"

"Yes!"

"Do you remember when the Pharisees asked Jesus if they should pay the tax to Caesar that the Jews felt was unjust and was used to promote injustice?"

The man looked trapped.

Jesus continued, "Did Jesus tell them that they should protest to change the law? Do you even remember what Jesus said?"

"Jesus told them to give to Caesar that which is Caesar's, and to give to God that which is God's."

"So that meant they were supposed to go protest the law?"

"No. It probably means something along the lines of going along with the earthly law but at the same time live in accordance with the higher law of God. But that was different. Those taxes weren't being used to fund abortions."

"Hmmm. Neither are yours. You do know your tax dollars have not been used to fund abortions since 1976, right? The Hyde Amendment prevents the use of federal dollars for abortions, except in cases of rape, or incest, or when the mother's life is at risk."

"But even given all that, people have killed doctors who performed abortions in order to uphold 'God's law' that killing is wrong. Does that make sense to you?"

"No, of course not! We don't support violence."

"Well, you are physically blocking the door, and that is likely to result in violence at some point. And you know the Constitution of the United States says people do not have to believe in the God you believe in. So are you trying to force people to believe in your God? Like the Christian Taliban or something, punish them if they don't repent?"

"We don't believe in forcing people to believe. But we do believe the baby has rights, too."

"And I think we have established that laws are not the best way to stop the behaviors that you are trying to stop, and that violence is not

the best way to turn people's hearts to the God you claim to be following. We are going to walk inside now, and I want you to let us in."

Jesus half turned and motioned me to lead into the crowd toward the
entrance. The crowd parted in front of me, Jane followed close behind,
and Jesus came in last.

He stopped at the doorway and turned back to the crowd. "I don't
disagree with what you are trying to accomplish—to protect innocent
life—but this thing you are doing here is not an effective way to achieve
that goal, and it's not what Jesus told you to do. Don't let others use
your love of your God to distract you from what is important and to
buy power for themselves."

University

Inside, across the lobby, I saw a window with a young woman sitting
in what appeared to be a larger administrative area. To the right rear of
the lobby, another door seemed the only way into the rest of the building. Jane walked over to the window and told the woman that she had
an appointment. The woman handed her a clipboard that looked like
the obligatory questionnaires and consent forms.

Holding the clipboard and pen in her left hand, Jane turned to Jesus
and I, "Thank you both. I don't know how I would have navigated that
without you."

"No worries. We're going to leave you for now, but call us when
you're done and we'll pick you up. You can stay at the shelter as long as
you need to stay. Don't feel pressured to rush into anything."

"Thank you."

No one blocked our path or said anything as we exited the clinic,
crossed the street, and climbed in the van. I emptied the dogs' water
dish so it wouldn't spill when the van started to move. Jesus pulled out
of his parking spot and merged into light traffic, still heading north.

"The hospital is actually a medical center on the campus of Green
Valley University. We can park there, but you don't need to stay with
me. I think you should head to the Behavioral Sciences Building and

describe your situation to them. They are the most likely ones to have some idea of what you can do to get home. Socrates and Plato can go with you, but you'll have to use a leash."

He turned right onto the campus, and proceeded along a tree-lined street that looped back toward the south. Just past a sign that read "Green Valley University Medical Center," he pulled into a parking garage and parked in the first empty stall on the second level.

We climbed out. I clipped leashes onto the dogs' collars, and we all headed for the stairwell in the corner. Jesus pulled up short and pointed to the northeast over a chest-high concrete wall.

"That red brick building is the Behavioral Sciences Department," he said. "Ask for Professor Karen Gautama, and tell her I sent you. She volunteers at the food bank sometimes. I'll follow you over there when I finish here. It shouldn't take me long. There's only so much they'll let me do, with the virus and all."

"That must be the virus line there," I said, pointing to a long line snaking out of the emergency room.

"Actually, no," Jesus said, indicating a shorter line leading into a white vinyl tent that stood in front of the main entrance. "The line going into that white tent is for virus testing and admissions. They call the other line the Bleach Eaters' line. It's for people who watch President Dumb's press conference and follow his non-medical medical advice."

The dogs and I followed Jesus into the stairwell. Even through the mask, I could smell the damp, cool concrete. We exited the garage at ground level, immediately crossing the U-shaped driveway that curved off the campus road in front of the main entrance and the emergency room entrance before curving back to merge with the street.

Jesus waved and headed off to the half left towards the white tent. The dogs and I broke to the right, following the sidewalk that paralleled the campus drive in the direction of the building Jesus had pointed out.

"I feel a little weird keeping you two on a leash," I said.

"No worries, we are used to it," Socrates replied.

"Yeah," Plato agreed. "I do need to pee, though, so how about stopping for a minute by this next big tree?"

"Sure."

Plato lifted his leg and doused the trunk thoroughly, then sauntered back onto the sidewalk. They continued on in silence. As they drew near to the red brick building, I saw a sign that read, "Department of Behavioral Sciences." Socrates took this opportunity to pee on one of the posts supporting the sign. Then all three of us walked up a ramp and turned right to enter the front door of the building.

A piece of paper taped to the glass on the inside of the door informed them that "All visitors must wear face coverings." Inside, the lobby was cool, with clean black tile on the floor. Opposite the entrance, two sets of double doors looked like they led to an auditorium. More doors flanked the lobby, one on each side. All the doors were locked.

An intercom was mounted near the door on the right-side wall, which also featured a glass-encased, black-felt board on which administrative and faculty room assignments were displayed with white lettering. Nearby, a metal-framed stand displayed a placard that read, "Due to the pandemic, all visitors must have an appointment." The left side of the lobby was dominated by photographs of the university leadership and department faculty.

A clock on the wall told me it was already 10:45. I pressed the button next to the intercom and said hello. A man's voice answered.

"Hi. Can I help you?"

"Yes, I would like to speak with Dr. Gautama, please. A friend from the food bank suggested we speak."

"Do you have an appointment?"

"No."

"Well, all visitors need appointments."

"When is the next available appointment?"

"11 o'clock, but since that is so close, I will have to check with Dr. Gautama first."

"Okay, please check. Tell her a mutual friend from the food bank suggested we meet. It's kind of urgent."

"Okay, I'll be right back."

I crossed the lobby and scanned the photographs until I found Professor Gautama's picture. From the face that stared back at me from the bank of pictures, I guessed she was forty-something. And, according to the short description, she held the Wanda B. Mucketymuck Chair of Behavioral Psychology. Dark hair and eyes, friendly smile... A metallic click behind me drew my attention back to the doorway next to the intercom. The door was now open, revealing a young man with reddish-blond hair and a thick beard behind a green mask bearing the university logo.

"Follow me, please. Professor Gautama is just finishing up some interviews, but you can wait in the admin area until she's ready."

I crossed the lobby, dogs in tow. He eyed them suspiciously but made no attempt to stop them from coming into the hallway that extended beyond the door.

We followed the young man into an office on the right-hand side of the hallway. The room was split by a counter that ran three-quarters of the way across the room from the far wall. A couple of desks were positioned on the far side, to the right of the counter from where we entered the room. Chairs lined the three walls from the door, wrapping around the room to their left and ending where the counter joined the wall.

I crossed the room and sat facing the door. No sooner had I seated myself when, through the open door, I heard noise coming from the hallway. A small group of people passed, heading for the exit. One man stepped into the office long enough to throw his mask on the counter. I could see a political slogan on his red MAMGTIEW hat, with letters starting in the front and extending all the way around his head.

"You can have that back. I don't need it."

He turned and nodded at me as he left. I noticed his shirt bore the same slogan as his hat: "Make America More Glorious Than It Ever Was."

Shortly after the metallic click signalled the last of the interviewees had left, Professor Gautama stuck her head in the office. Seeing me, she entered and crossed the room as I rose from my chair. She waved her hand confidently, in a virus-safe greeting, with the same friendly smile I recognized from the lobby picture.

"Hi. I'm Professor Gautama. Call me Karen."

"Hello, I'm Stephen. Jesus, from the food bank, should be here soon as well. He was the one who suggested I ask for your help."

"Oh, yeah, I've worked with him before. Do you volunteer at the food bank?"

"Well, not really, but that's kind of why I need your help."

"And who are these two?" She reached down and scratched each dog on the head.

To my surprise, the older dog spoke up. "I'm Socrates, and this is Plato."

"Wow! Great names!" Gautama did not seem at all surprised that the dogs could speak.

"Cucullus non fakit monachem, Professor, as I'm sure you well know." Socrates pulled his lips back to show just a little of his teeth, a gesture I now recognized as a grin.

Gautama laughed, "You even speak Latin. Very impressive. And what about you, Mr. Plato?"

"Well, I follow my teacher's lead, mostly, but I do have a few Ideas of my own."

"I'll bet you do." She laughed again. "Let's go back to my office."

Turning to the young man behind the counter, she added, "Jerry, there's one more coming. Please bring him right back to my office when he arrives."

Karen led the way into the hallway, turned right, then left down another hallway. At the end of that hallway, she climbed a flight of stairs, then turned back into the hallway, and immediately left into a spacious, well-furnished office with restful views of oak trees outside the windows.

"I tell my students that finding my office is a cognitive test like the mazes we use for rats," she joked.

The room was appointed in dark wood, and shelves filled with books were built in to the walls. There was a leather couch and two arm chairs flanking a coffee table. Behind that, next to the windows, was a large mahogany desk. Karen grabbed some waters from a refrigerator near the desk. She handed one to me, poured another in a bowl for the dogs, kept one for herself, and set an extra on the coffee table. Then she sat at one end of the couch, while I took the arm chair closest to her, and the dogs settled on the rug in front of the coffee table.

"Looks like you had quite a crew in here this morning. Was that some kind of political group?"

"Oh, yes, they were in some classrooms on the first floor. With the election this year, we're taking every opportunity to have focus groups in to complete surveys on their views and behaviors. Since President Dumb is having a rally here in Green Valley tomorrow, today was a good chance to get information from the people that have come into town to see him."

"I confess I have opposed Dumb ever since he announced he was running for president. I just could never understand how we could elect someone with his record as a bully, a liar and a draft dodger."

"Well, it has been interesting to watch the profile of his supporters change over time," Karen said. "A common perception among many voters across the spectrum for the past fifteen years has been the sense that our federal government is failing us—that it no longer responds to the wishes of the people. Originally, among Dumb supporters, there was a segment that viewed Dumb as the solution to this problem: Dumb was the capitalist iconoclast who would go to Washington, break the bureaucracy, and restore simple, effective government."

Karen paused, took a sip of water, and continued. "Many of these people have now abandoned Dumb, including prominent members of his first cabinet who didn't really know him until they saw him up close from inside the administration."

"Among the rational voters who remain loyal to the president are those who either can't admit they were wrong or who still do not believe they were wrong. This last group includes the Christians who have traded support for Dumb to get conservative judges they think will overturn the laws allowing abortion. There is another group that supports the president out of naked self interest. That's not charming, but at least it's rational. The other segments of his original base are more troubling."

"How so? I know why I find them troubling, but I'm curious as to what your surveys show."

"Well, if you take the original base, with that perception of the federal government as failing them, and then you remove the percentage who viewed Dumb as a reasonable choice for some reason, you are left with those who chose Dumb based on emotion rather than reason. At the low end of this spectrum, the emotion is hate. This is where you find your racists, your white nationalists, and your sociopaths. Higher up on the spectrum of emotion-based supporters, you find people who are unhappy with their lives and their level of personal achievement compared with some others. Many of these people get emotional satisfaction from the the fact that Dumb gives them someone to blame for the way their lives have turned out."

"They don't want to blame themselves, so they like Dumb because he tells them it's the immigrants, the media, the liberals and the mythical 'deep state' that have conspired to blow up the American dream. And when they all come together in a rally, you see some people who simply feel good about being a part of something. They feel like they belong when they are with Dumb people."

"Wow. That is really interesting, and a bit scary," I said. "You mentioned some people at the low end of the rational spectrum who support Dumb purely out of self interest. What can you say about that group?"

"Well, for one thing, I think we were all surprised by how big it is. I think many of us thought that would just be the Roger Rocks of the world—bazillion-heir misfits with tattoos of King George on their backs, absorbed in some juvenile fantasy about how they would be princes in a new world order without the constraints of the rule of law. But I think we were all shocked at how many came out of the woodwork, willing to sell their services to Dumb for the right price—

senators and attorney gerbils and governors and cabinet secretaries and even generals like McFinn."

"Goodness! It seems a big mess. How do we fix it, I wonder?"

Socrates spoke up from the rug. "In my time, I saw Athens' democracy decay into corruption and the rule of the mob. That seems to be what you are describing. I do not pretend to know the answer, but perhaps it is the nature of democracy to decay in this manner?"

"But you did not have the information technology systems we have at our disposal today," I said. "It seems to me that we should be able to build systems that give every citizen enough information to make wise social choices. Of course, individual choices will always be flawed, to a greater or lesser extent, by individual bias. But here again, we have the information systems to aggregate the choices of individuals in a way that allows us to tap the wisdom of crowds without falling prey to the rule of the mob."

Plato spoke up in response, "My view is that only a select few will have the ability or inclination to take advantage of your information systems to gain true wisdom. That is why I thought society should be built to train those people to lead the state."

"I think you underestimate the power of information systems. We can gamify and reward the process of high-quality engagement by a large number of citizens. I think this is the way forward for an enlightened 21st-century republic."

"One dog's enlightenment is another dog's tyranny. Even with the systems you speak of, what other reforms would be necessary to keep the delicate balance between the wisdom of crowds and the rule of the mob?"

"That is a great question, Plato. I can suggest some off the top of my head, like minimizing private money in politics and building fair districts for representation based on balancing different philosophies. But I'm sure there are many others."

Professor Gautama interjected, "You know, I have a video conference this evening with senior faculty members from both our computer science department and our political science department. Maybe you all should come to that? I'm sure the venue will allow us to keep appropriate social distance and still include you all."

A knock on the door interrupted their conversation. Jerry stuck his head in. "Your other guest is here, Professor."

"Thank you, Jerry."

The door opened the rest of the way, and Jesus came in, a big smile on his face.

"Hello, Jesus! So good to see you. Come, have a seat. That water is for you," Karen motioned at the bottle on the coffee table.

"Hi, Professor!" He entered and took a seat on the couch, throwing air "fist bumps" at me, Karen and the dogs.

Socrates gave a low "woof" in greeting.

"Thanks for seeing my friends and I. Have you made any progress?"

"Oh, I am sorry," I said, "I have kept the Professor busy with questions about her research. We haven't even started talking about my stuff yet."

Professor Gautama looked at me quizzically.

"I'm not from Green Valley, Professor. Truth be told, I don't know how I got here. I woke up in front of Socrates' dog house."

"Very interesting. What's the last thing you remember from before Green Valley?"

"I was having a dream," I said, and recounted my first adventure as a moth in the Oval Office.

"Where were you before the dream?" she asked.

It seemed an eternity since I was reading in my den, but her eyes lit up when I described my late-night studies in information systems.

"If you suddenly woke up and found yourself studying information systems, would you feel like you were 'home', or is there another level you haven't told me about?"

"No, I think that was home. I don't remember anything before that."

"Socrates, did you hear or see anything strange before you found Stephen in your yard? What happened next?"

Socrates thought for a moment. "No, I'm a pretty heavy sleeper these days. I just woke up as I normally do in the morning, walked outside to get a drink of water, and found Stephen laying on my toy." He went on to relate the encounter with the ICE raven and journey to the model makers' workshop. Plato and Jesus chimed in to add their parts of the story, bringing us right up to the present.

"Oh, and one other thing," I said. "I had another dream last night about eavesdropping in the Oval Office. I heard President Dumb talking about a rally in Green Valley. Then today, after I woke up, I found out there really is going to be a rally here. Pretty sure I had not heard about it before my dream, though."

"Hmmm. Of course you are eager to get back home, and preferably before you have to show up in court?"

"Yes, absolutely."

"Well, good news, I think. Dreams are often where our minds work to resolve issues we are experiencing in our waking lives. When we were first discussing my surveys of President Dumb's supporters, you were quite eager to chime in with your ideas on using information systems to solve political problems like engagement and gridlock and corruption. It seems likely to me that is the root of your dream experience—your desire to bring your studies to bear on the real problems of politics.

If we give you a forum where you can fully present and work through your solutions, then the seed of the original dream may be satisfied, allowing you to wake up. I think it is important that you come to the seminar this evening prepared to present a couple of your ideas about how we can use information systems to make government work better. We start at seven in the auditorium on the first floor. What do you think?"

For the first time in days, I felt like I could see a way out of my predicament.

"Thank you," I said. "This gives me hope."

Turning to Jesus, I added, "Can you get me back here for the seminar tonight, or should I just stay here now?"

"I'll bring you back," Jesus said, glancing at his watch. "For now, though, we should probably be on our way. I have an errand to run down on Embassy Row, and Jane should be finished with her appointment before too much longer as well."

The group walked downstairs, with Professor Gautama in the lead. She stuck her head in the office, "Jerry, please unlock the door so our guests can leave. They will be coming back for our seminar this evening. Please see to it they get seated appropriately in the participant sections."

"All right, Professor. Also, I wanted to remind you I have jury duty the day after tomorrow."

"That's right! Thanks for reminding me," she said. Then, to us, "See you in a bit."

Grateful for what seemed a rational way back to my life, I said to Professor Gautama, "Professor, I can't thank you enough! We'll see you tonight."

Jesus and I and the dogs walked back across campus, savoring the scenery and the fresh air. Crossing in front of the hospital, we climbed the stairs back to our van. Jesus backed out and drove carefully down the ramp, back out to campus drive, and to the university exit. This time I noted the name of the road we turned on as we left the university: El Camino Real. We turned north, heading still further away from the shelter.

"This should be a quick errand," Jesus said. In a couple blocks, he turned eastward onto a street named Embassy Row. After maybe three blocks on this road, he brought the vehicle to rest at the curb in front of a sign that read "Embassy of the State of Israel."

He got out. I joined him, and we walked over to the security post just outside the gate. A distinguished-looking hispanic man in blue security uniform stepped outside as they approached. He was wearing a black face mask.

"Hi, I'm Jesus from the food bank. My friend Sam Myer called and asked me to come by to see him. He said he had something for me."

"Ok, we'll give him a call. Wait here, please." He turned back toward the guard post, where another guard had appeared in the doorway and was watching them closely. "Please call Mr. Myer and tell him he has visitors from the food bank."

A few moments later, a thick, well-muscled man with curly black hair approached the gate from the direction of the main embassy building. He carried a canvas tote that appeared to be heavy.

"Hi, Jesus." He nodded at me as well. "Hello, I'm Sam Myer."

"Hey, Sam, thanks for thinking of us," Jesus said.

"Eh, might as well make something good of this. That putz of a president of yours sends a Barry and Goliath ham to the Israeli Embassy on the occasion of the Prime Minister's birthday 'with his compliments.' Who doesn't know that ham isn't kosher? The ambassador was pretty angry, but I calmed him down. You can use this at the food bank, right?"

"Yes, of course. Sorry about the odd gift. Really don't know how to explain our President Dumb."

"No worries. All's well that ends well. At least the ham won't go to waste."

"You're right about that!" Jesus said.

Gladimeer's Embassy

As we turned away from the security post, another embassy across the street caught my attention. The left side of the structure was almost a mirror image of the Israeli Embassy. To the right, however, the grounds looked more like a cheap casino. A bright neon sign blinked on and off over the rear exit to the compound. The sign read "Gladimeer's."

While they were taking in the bizarre contrast between the two sides of the compound, a door opened under the neon sign and two men emerged in suits. Behind them in the open doorway, flashing disco lights and pulsating music sprayed festively into the night.

Neither man wore a mask, allowing me to see their features with perfect clarity. I recognized them both from the news. It was none other than Senator Turtlechin M. Cracker and his Republican colleague Senator Graham Cracker. Both men looked around furtively, and started walking quickly north away from the compound, as if they didn't want to be seen.

Behind them, the door opened again. This time a short, balding man with no shirt and a camera slung around his neck hurried out to the street. He yelled after the two retreating senators, "Hey, guys, you were going to leave without saying goodbye? I hope you had a good time. Did you choose your picture package?"

I recognized this newcomer as Gladimeer Lillipootin, President of the Fallopian Federation.

The two senators waved their hands as if to push Lillipootin back inside with whatever wind they could generate. They said something, but I couldn't make it out.

"Oh, you guys and your modesty! You're really too much! Well, we'll just hold your pictures in case you change your mind. No charge!"

Turning back toward the door from which he had come, he saw us across the street and waved. "Hey guys, how are you? You wanna ditch those masks and come have some fun?"

"No, we're in a hurry to meet a friend," Jesus said.

I couldn't resist a question. "Was that really Turtlechin M. Cracker and Graham Cracker from the Senate?"

"Yes, those two are here all the time! I don't know why they wanted to sneak off like that, without even saying goodbye. They were feeling a little sheepish today, I think."

"Let's go," Jesus said, turning and climbing back in the van. I walked to my side and got in.

"Sorry," he said. "Bad vibe with that place."

Jesus started the van, made two right turns and then a left onto Camino Real. Now they were heading south, back towards the clinic and the shelter. His phone chirped from the cup holder where he had set it.

"Will you answer that, please?" he asked.

"Sure." I picked it up. Jane was calling to say she was ready to return to the shelter. I told her we were on our way and would be at the clinic in a few minutes.

There was still a group of protesters picketing outside the clinic when Jesus pulled up. I got out and walked in to meet Jane, then escorted her back to the van without incident.

Back at the shelter, Jesus just had time to get dinner organized. He enlisted help from some of the other residents and staff to serve the meal. He and I were the first through the line. We ate quickly, made sure the dogs were fed, and then the four of us headed back to the university for the seminar. This time, Jesus parked in the visitor lot outside the Behavioral Sciences building.

Seminar

We checked in with Jerry inside, and he had another student guide us into the auditorium and to our seats. There were only a few people attending the event live, all in masks and well spaced out. Our guide seated us in the front row on the right side, near where a podium for audience questions and comments was positioned.

On the stage, a man I did not recognize stood behind another podium. Several faculty members, including Professor Gautama, sat behind a long table in the center of the stage. There were water bottles and microphones in front of each of the panelists.

"Good evening," the man behind the podium said. I am Professor Ted Waterman of the Department of Behavioral Sciences. Tonight, we have a distinguished panel of faculty from our Behavioral Sciences, Information Technology and Political Sciences departments. In light of President Dumb's rally here in Green Valley tomorrow, not to mention the Black Lives Matter rally at the courthouse, we thought it appropriate to schedule this special interdisciplinary seminar with the topic of "21st Century Governance for the American Republic." This is an online seminar in partial fulfillment of week 13 requirements for the courses shown here."

The speaker used a laser pointer to draw their attention to a slide with seven or eight courses listed. Advancing the presentation to the next slide, he continued: "Here is our agenda."

The items listed included introductions, purposes of government, technology and government, the psychology of political bias, visiting scholar comments, and questions.

"You may submit questions using the chat function, and we will try to answer as many as possible. Without further delay, I will ask each member of our panel to introduce themselves and we'll begin. Professor Gautama, may I ask you to start us off?"

Karen spoke briefly about her background and how her recent work on the psychology of political alignment had led to her participation on today's panel.

Next, Professor Donald Byteme from the Computer Science department introduced himself, noting how his interest in blockchain and electronic voting technology had prompted him to sign up for this panel. Last to speak was Professor Constance Tooshen of the Political Science department. Professor Tooshen stated that her research in the relationship between forms of government, quantity of regulations, and citizen satisfaction led to her invitation to join this panel.

Professor Tooshen kicked off the panel discussion. "The Constitution lists six purposes for the American government right at the beginning. They are to form a more perfect union, establish justice, insure domestic tranquility, provide for the common defense, promote the general welfare, and secure the blessings of liberty to ourselves and our posterity. In recent years, many Americans have become disillusioned with the government's ability to accomplish these purposes. Many view the election of President Dumb as a backlash against ineffective government. Given the 2016 election, the turbulence of the past several years, and the pandemic, it is reasonable for us to consider to what degree the government was failing before the 2016 election, whether the current administration has made things better or worse, and what we can do to adapt our government for the 21st century."

After about ten minutes, Professor Tooshen concluded her remarks, and Professor Donald Byteme took over, making general comments about how information technology could safely and securely enable elections, remote sessions of legislative bodies, and citizen engagement activities. Professor Gautama spoke last.

"As we told you at the beginning of the evening, I am a behavioral scientist, and Professor Tooshen is a political scientist, and Donald Byteme is a computer scientist. We are scientists because we use the scientific method to pursue truth. We use time-tested standards for telling whether a theory is true or false. The theories rely on propositions that must be able to be proven false, and we assess whether those propositions are true or false based on whether they predict future outcomes, whether the outcomes they predict are repeatable, whether the propositions correspond to and are coherent with the world we experience."

"We are challenged because we know, through reproducible research, that almost all of us, almost all of the time, see the world inaccurately to some degree because of cognitive bias—systemic patterns of deviation from the norm and from rational judgment. This bias can take many forms.

There is confirmation bias, which is the tendency to see evidence in a way that confirms our preconceptions. There is anchoring, or the tendency to not adjust our belief to the degree that new evidence tells us we should. There is availability bias, which is the tendency to overestimate the likelihood of events that are most common in our memory. There are phantom patterns, or the tendency to overemphasize the importance of small streaks or clusters in large samples of random data. And there are more."

"Given all these natural tendencies to see things in a distorted way, we must work at overcoming our cognitive bias. We can do this by making a habit of consulting multiple, legitimate sources of news with different perspectives. We have to make a habit of exposing ourselves to diversity and diverse opinions on controversial subjects. We should make an effort to cultivate relationships with people who look and think differently than we do. Ultimately, we should consider the perspectives of other people as often as we can."

"There may be no more compelling evidence that we are social animals than the fact that we need each other to achieve a reasonable standard of truth in many cases. We cannot be sure we are seeing the world correctly without the ability to check each other's blind spots. We cannot be sure we are reacting appropriately to new evidence without confirming with others that the new evidence corresponds with the world the way we think it does, and that it is coherent with other relevant evidence. The ancients were right—even though individuals have the ability to deny our nature in word and deed, often for their own selfish ends—our nature is inherently social."

Socrates and Plato both smiled at that.

She concluded by noting that many of President Dumb's supporters used 'socialism' as a negative label to condemn anything that they felt infringed on their individual liberty. She noted that the real definition of socialism—an economic system wherein the government owned the means of production—was not always appropriate for the many different ways the label was used. She observed that the United States was a hybrid system with a mostly capitalist economy but with some socialist elements, such as the Veterans Administration health system, or, for that matter, the United States military. And she stated her opinion that a hybrid system has a distinct advantage because different types of challenges can be handled best by either a free-market solution, a government solution, or a mix of both. Using 'socialism' as a negative political label, she said, undermines the power we gain from seeing ourselves as fundamentally social animals and attacks the very foundations of knowledge and truth.

Then she turned to the podium. "That concludes my remarks, Professor Waterman. However, I have asked a visiting scholar to prepare a few remarks for the panel's consideration, and I think now would be a good time for him to share his ideas with us. Stephen, are you ready?"

I left my seat, and moved to the podium.

"Thank you, Professor. The hypothesis I present for your consideration is that the root cause of the dissatisfaction with our government--dissatisfaction you have all acknowledged—is that the information-age requirements for effective citizenship have dramatically outpaced the tools and systems available for citizens in our society. As a starting point, we should redesign our congressional districts so they balance opposing political philosophies as much as possible. That will make every voter feel their vote is important, and will increase engagement."

I was pleased to see my premise drew a positive reaction from Donald Byteme.

"Next, there is the information problem. The volume of information is overwhelming. The quality of that information varies from very poor to very good. Many people simply don't have the skills or the time to filter the information they consume. So they default to trusted institutions, like their church, political party, family and friends. Bad actors abuse the trust people have in these institutions with overly simplistic models that support ulterior motives. This is especially true for religious and political organizations. We have to give people tools that enable them to filter low-quality information, an incentive to spend time refining their personal positions on key issues, and a nonthreatening way to evaluate different perspectives."

"My proposal is something I call Congress 2.0: realigning Congress' information systems and processes to increase transparency and informed engagement with the citizens that Members of Congress are supposed to represent. Congressional web sites should leverage the technologies described by Donald Byteme. Specifically, those web sites should incorporate real-time collaboration and survey tools, secured by blockchain, encryption and audits. These systems should provide full visibility for all registered voters."

I continued with a brief overview of a web site architecture that could support Congress 2.0. and a use case that walked the audience through one citizen's engagement with one issue. The web site would allow registered voters to sign in and see a summary view of current voter sentiments in their state. The tools for evaluating alternative positions and registering or updating a preference would all be simple clicks from the home page. I concluded by noting that, since all the technology is commercially available now, there is no reason why these web sites could not be live in a few months.

The panel nodded approvingly, especially Donald Byteme.

Professor Gautama gave the first reaction from the panel. "Very nicely done, Stephen, thank you. I can confirm that our research into the psychology of voters shows that a big reason for voter apathy is the fact that our current districts effectively disenfranchise voters from one party or the other."

"I think about 400 of the 435 congressional districts are so lopsided one way or the other that many voters just assume their vote won't count. Redistricting to eliminate these artificial, gerrymandered majority districts would improve voter engagement and participation."

Professor Tooshen chimed in with her support as well. "Yes, the Supreme Court has ruled consistently that districts must not disenfranchise voters. The original case was Baker v. Carr, I think, but there have been recent cases as well. And there are bipartisan groups all across the country calling for fairer redistricting based on the 2020 census."

Finally it was time for the comments of the panelist from the Computer Science department. "Two thumbs up. We could build the web sites you describe using existing technology in just a few months, and it wouldn't even be very expensive," said Donald Byteme.

I returned to my seat. Jesus, Socrates, and Plato nodded approvingly. The rest of the questions and answers were a blur for me. I was relieved to have presented my ideas to the seminar, and gratified to have the panel express strong approval.

The seminar ended just after 9 o'clock. We said thank you to Professor Gautama and the other panelists, and bid them good night.

On the way to the shelter, Jesus asked my opinion on Professor Gautama's comments. I told him I thought the attempt to confuse our social nature with the negative connotations of tyrannical, dystopian socialist economic systems was a serious threat. He seemed energized by my comments on how the Old Testament story of the Tower of Babel could be an effective way to address that threat.

"That is interesting. Please explain."

"Well, the traditional interpretation of the Babel story is that God saw humans cooperating to build a tower to heaven. So he confused their languages to prevent them from completing the tower. The story is used as a description of why there are these differences between peoples. It's odd that in this story, God is trying to keep us out of heaven."

"Go on."

"Jesus' great commandment offers us a way to interpret the story as a prescription for how to build the tower by learning to love our neighbors as ourselves. By accepting those who are different, and finding a way to use every person's brick, we can finish the tower and find our way to God together. Put a slightly different way, our salvation is not dependent on having our view of God prevail over others' views, but rather finding the way our different views can be complementary to one another."

Then, as we walked from the parking lot into the shelter, the conversation turned to the schedule of events for the following day. I agreed to attend the Black Lives Matter rally in the morning. Secretly, I hoped Professor Gautama's theory about my dream was correct, and that I would wake up in my study at home rather than in the Green Valley Shelter. Nevertheless, I agreed to help Jesus serve breakfast in the morning, and set my alarm before the dogs and I settled down for the night.

CHAPTER 4

Bureaucracy Games, and How I Got Arrested

The president's voice told me I was back in the Oval Office, and back in my dream.

"What the hell!" President Dumb exclaimed. "We're under attack! Get me to the bunker!"

Weapons drawn, two secret service agents rushed over to where the president cowered under the big desk.

One positioned himself between the president and the semicircle of windows behind the desk. The other leaned over and extended his hand.

It's okay, Mr. President, we're not under attack. I guarantee it." The agent who offered his hand spoke calmly. "Something knocked over a vase, that's all. Looked like a bird."

Meanwhile, on the floor where I had just landed after knocking over the vase, my heart was pounding. I tried to fly away to keep from being caught, only to discover that I had six legs and zero lift. Fortunately, I had shrunk back down to the size of a bug again, but the best I could do was scuttle away under the small cabinet from which the vase had fallen. I clambered up one of the legs closest to the wall, coming to rest on the backside of the cabinet, positioned so I could still see the agent trying to calm the president.

"Believe me, sir, I've been under attack a bunch, and this ain't it."

"Well, get that damned bird out of here!" President Dumb thundered.

"Yes, sir."

The administrative staff had responded to the noise, and were already busy cleaning up the mess caused by the shattered vase. The Attorney Gerbil had rolled himself over onto his back and was trying to elbow himself back to a seated position. One of the staff reached down and helped him roll over onto his knees, and then to his feet.

"Mr. President, if you have nothing further, I am going to head back over to Justice now," he wheezed.

"Okay, DamLow, just make sure you are with me for the rally in Green Valley tomorrow. I need my DamLow Bar to make it a success."

"Yes, Mr. President."

Another Bright Idea

"Paul, what are we going to do? You know one of my disloyal staff is leaking this to the press. It's another embarrassing incident."

"I've been thinking about just that thing, Mr. President. I think we should say you came under attack by an ANTIFA drone."

"Hey, I like that! And then we say I saved the lives of several of my staff, including the Attorney Gerbil, by throwing a vase at the drone and destroying it."

"What will we say when people want to see it?"

"We just tell them it's been sent to a top secret laboratory for analysis, and the results will be classified top secret, like all my conversations with Gladimeer. Or other foreign leaders when I'm talking about my properties in their countries."

"Right! Brilliant, Mr. President."

"Do you think I can give myself the Presidential Medal of Freedom for this?"

"It would be pretty awkward, sir. I mean, how would you present it to yourself? It would be harder than drinking a glass of water, and you only have two hands... but you could have Senator Cracker present you with something like a Congressional Gold Medal... we could even do that at the rally tomorrow!"

"Good thinking, Paul!" The president hit the intercom on his desk. "Get Bitch Cracker on the phone right away!"

"Who, sir?"

"Bitch Cracker, you know, the Senate Majority Leader!"

"Yes, sir."

A moment later the intercom crackled. "Sir, Senator Cracker is on the phone for you."

The president picked up the phone and hit the button to make the connection, putting the conversation on speaker phone.

"Bitch, this is President Dumb. Did you hear we were attacked by an ANTIFA drone over here?"

"Why no, Mr. President. Are you okay?"

"I'm better than okay. I saved my staff by throwing a vase at the drone and destroying it. I'm a hero."

"He did! He really did!" Paul Pasturepie chimed in.

"That's, ah, good news, Mr. President."

"Paul thinks you should award me the Congressional Gold Medal at my rally in Green Valley tomorrow."

"Uh, We'll never get Fancy Paloozi and the House to pass the Act of Congress for a Congressional Gold Medal, but we could award you the Senate half. You would be the first person in history to get that... Ah guess we could do that."

"Very good. I'm going to send Paul over to coordinate everything with you directly. And, by the way, Gladimeer tells me he's got some pictures for you. Do you want me to have him bring them to the rally?"

"No, Mr. President, please don't do that. And tell Paul we are working on the new virus relief package this afternoon, so Ah will be on the Senate floor from time to time."

"Ok, great, any other ideas on what I should say at the rally?"

"Ah think you should get one of the big telly Christians to come... you know, like Banklyn Ham? The medal thing will check the mindless patriotism block, but we need somebody to check the Christian block.

And thank God none of Banklyn's flock can read or understand the gospels for themselves."

"Good idea, Bitch, we'll reach out to him right away."

"And Mr. President, could you please call me 'Mitch'. Mah name is Turtlechin M. Cracker, and the 'M' stands for Mitch."

"Yeah, that's what I said, Bitch. And you did say no on the pictures, right?"

"Uh, yes, that's right, Mr. President."

"Good. Paul will be over to talk to you in a little bit."

The president hung up the phone and looked over at his chief of staff. "Did you get all that?"

"Yes, sir. You may want to have Ibetya talk to Banklyn Ham. It will take me the rest of the day to manage the Congressional Gold Medal."

"Okay, let's get her in here for a few minutes before you leave." He hit the intercom and summoned his daughter.

Ibetya Dumb

While President Dumb and Paul Pasturepie were waiting, I crawled down the leg of the cabinet and headed across the room towards where Pasturepie sat. I wanted to be with him when he went to the Senate. By this time, I had figured out I was a small, six-legged insect, like maybe a ladybug. After a series of short hops, I positioned myself on the rear of his suit jacket, near the collar.

Ibetya Dumb bounced into the room. "Hi, Daddy!"

"Ibetya! My favorite. Come sit on daddy's lap."

Ibetya skipped behind the big desk and perched on Dumb's knee, one arm draped around his neck and her head cocked sideways. "How is your day going, Daddy?"

"Very well, Ibetya. Did you hear that I saved my staff from an ANTIFA drone attack?"

"No! Daddy, you're so brave! ANTIFA is so bad!"

"They are bad. Nasty people. They all work for Celery, and you know how bad she is."

"Yes, I do! I remember you told me she had your friend Jeremy Creepstein killed. He was such a nice man. Remember when you sent me to his house for a play date?"

"I certainly do. I had a play date at the same time. Talk about The Art of the Wheel!"

"I need you to do something to help me get ready for my big rally tomorrow. I need you to call Banklyn Ham and have him come, give the opening prayer and endorse me. Then Senator Cracker is going to present me with a special medal for my victory over ANTIFA. It will be a great day!"

"Of course, daddy. Can I come to the rally?"

"Yes, I want you to take care of getting Banklyn there. Make all the arrangements and accompany him."

"That will be easy!"

"Paul, you better head over to talk to Senator Cracker now. That's all for you both. I have some twitter stuff to do... have to let the world know about the battle of the oval office. He pulled out his cell phone as Paul Pasturepie and Ibetya Dumb walked out.

Senators at Work

Riding on Paul Pasturepie's back was a little unstable, and I found I needed all six of my legs to maintain my perch as he walked. I heard him ask the administrative staff to have a car sent around to take him to the Capitol, and to notify the Leader's office that he was on the way. He instructed an aide to reschedule his appointments for the next three hours, and headed out onto West Executive Avenue Northwest to meet his car. He told the driver to take him to the north wing of the Capitol.

The driver weaved his way expertly through the traffic, turning left onto Pennsylvania Avenue and negotiating a labyrinth of one-way streets before stopping in front of a massive concrete and steel barrier near some special access parking off East Capitol Drive. One of Senator Cracker's aides met Pasturepie as he passed through security at the entrance.

"Sir, Senator Cracker is on the floor for consideration of the latest virus relief package. He asked me to bring you to the balcony so you can watch if you wish. He said something about a Senate Gold Medal for the President. Perhaps you can rough out the words you want on the citation while you wait?"

"Let's do that first."

"I have some paper here. You can sit in the old Supreme Court chamber if you wish."

"Perfect."

Pasturepie followed the aide into the room where the Supreme Court had met for most of the nineteenth century. He sat, took the paper offered by the aide, produced a pen from the inside pocket of his jacket, and began to write.

"The Senate of the United States hereby awards President Donnie Dumb the Senate Half of a Congressional Gold Medal for exceptionally meritorious service and the most extreme bravery ever in the history of the republic when, in response to a heinous and cowardly attack by an ANTIFA drone in the Oval Office, President Dumb did expose himself to said drone, not in an improper way, of course, but only so he could move to a side cabinet, quickly grab a priceless Ming vase, and hurl it at the drone, thereby saving the lives of countless people in the West Wing... yadda, yadda, yadda... how about that?"

"That works, sir. I will take care of the paperwork and ensure everything is ready for Senator Cracker to present the medal tomorrow at the rally." The aide led Pasturepie out into the hallway. On the way to the balcony, he took a short detour to the Senate Majority Leader's suite to pass the handwritten citation off to someone for preparation of the formal, typed certificate. Then he escorted Pasturepie, with me still the undetected stowaway, onto the balcony overlooking the Senate Chamber.

The scene below was bizarre, indeed. From my perch on Pasturepie's shoulder in the balcony, I could see the Majority Leader in the front of the chamber. To the right of the aisle below me were the desks of the Republican senators. On the far side of the aisle were the Democrats.

All the Republicans were dressed in red tights, while the Democrats wore blue. Both sides carried badminton racquets. The Majority Leader struck the podium with his gavel. He reminded everyone that, according to the rules, only the team serving could score points.

"And now, the National Anthem."

The Republicans all stood, placed their hands over their hearts and started to sing. "Oh, say can you see...."

Meanwhile , on the Democratic side of the aisle, everyone kneeled. Some held raised fists in the air. As the song reached its climax, tears were streaming down every Republican face. "...and the ho-ome of the----bra—aaave!"

Cheers erupted from the balcony. The senior senator from Utah, Tike Flea, tried to keep his party going, hopping sideways in front of his teammates, hands making rapid little circles towards the ceiling, as he sung lustily, "Row, row, row your boat, Gently down the streee-am!"

Cracker swung the gavel down sharply. "Order, order! Senator Flea, please, it's game time, suh!"

Striking the gavel again, he exclaimed, "Republicans have the serve!"

One of the red-clad senators dropped the virus-bill shuttlecock with his left hand. With his right hand, he gracefully swung his racquet to meet the rubber head of the "birdie." The twang of the racquet strings told everyone that it was a solid serve, and the shuttlecock arched grace-fully over the aisle.

The Democrats scrambled to respond. With an astonishing display of athleticism, Minority Leader Buck Schooner sprinted from the corner with racquet arm cocked, deftly tapping the shuttlecock toward a vacant area on the Republican side. Three Republicans converged on the descending birdie. One swung his racquet wildly, hitting a second in the head. The third tripped over the second, and all three tumbled together in a heap on the floor. The shuttlecock bounced just inside the line. A cheer erupted from the blue balcony.

"The Democrats have won the serve," the Majority Leader pro-nounced solemnly. "Raise the net!"

With a low hum, the net that had run at waist height down the aisle began to rise. The net rose all the way to the ceiling, making it impossible for the Democrats to get a serve across the aisle. A chorus of boos rained down on the Majority Leader.

"That's not fair!" someone shouted.

"Order, order!" he cried, striking his gavel. "We have rules in this chamber, and our rules are what separate us from the beasts! Senator Schooner, you may serve."

Schooner struck the shuttlecock, sending it to bounce inevitably backwards from the net and fall to the floor.

"The Republicans have won the serve!" Senator Cracker announced from his position at the front of the chamber. "Lower the net!"

Another Republican senator sent the shuttlecock flying towards Democratic space, only to have it pounded back by Senator Bory Cooker. In this fashion, the two sides traded serves for forty-five minutes, with neither side scoring any points.

Exasperated, Senator Cracker brought his gavel down sharply. "The Senate will adjourn for thirty minutes. Senator Schooner, please meet me in the cloakroom."

"Now's our chance," the aide exclaimed. "Let's see if we can get a few minutes with the senator in the cloakroom." They fought their way through clusters of lobbyists. Reaching the lower level, they made their way toward the cloakroom. As red and blue clad senators emerged from the chamber, lobbyists swarmed them like flies at a barbeque.

From the doorway to the cloakroom, they could see the Majority Leader and Senator Schooner standing together in a corner, talking earnestly. Floor staff kept everyone a respectful distance from the two. After a few minutes, both men started nodding their heads, as if some agreement had been struck. Their eyes locked in acknowledgement of whatever deal they had made, and the two men parted.

Paul Pasturepie stepped in front of the aide, seeming to remember his status as a former Member of Congress, "Leader Cracker," he addressed the Majority Leader.

"Hello, Paul, thanks for coming over. What's this about a Congressional Medal for the president?"

"The president is really getting hammered in the polls with all the bad news about the virus, Senator. We have more virus deaths now than from all the wars of the last seventy years combined, and more than any other country on earth. We need to make this rally a big win for President Dumb. I wrote a citation and gave it to your staff. We'll have Banklyn Ham give the invocation, then he will introduce you. Your part is just to say nice things about the president, then read the citation and hang the medal around his neck. Maybe get the rally going with some cheer, like "Four More Years," or "Lock Her Up! Really doesn't matter with this crowd, just something to hit 'em in the old "mindless patriotism" reflex. Then you're outta there."

"Okay, Ah can do that. Green Valley Stadium tomorrow afternoon, right? Ah'll be there about a quarter to one."

"Great, Senator, thank you! The President really appreciates this!"

"Okay, go back up to the balcony and watch this virus relief bill pass. Then you can go back and tell the President it's a done deal." Then, to his aide, "Once the one-pager on this bill is done, send it over to Paul so the President can use it in his remarks tomorrow."

With the aide leading the way, we made our way back upstairs. Republican senators were clustered on their side of the aisle, each with arms interlocked around the shoulders of the senators standing next to them. The Democrats were similarly postured on their side of the aisle.

Senator Cracker returned to the front of the chamber, seized the gavel, and, looking for all the world like Zeus on Xanax, rapped the podium.

"Reddd----dy, break!" Both groups of senators broke their huddles and resumed their playing positions, racquets in hand.

"The Senate will now come to order. Republicans have the serve."

One of the red-clad senators sent the shuttlecock sailing, in a now-familiar ritual. But this time, the Democrats did not respond. The stood with their racquets at their sides and watched as the birdie bounced on their side of the aisle.

"The bill is passed!" Cracker exclaimed, thwacking his gavel lustily.

"Let's get out of here," Pasturepie said to the aide, moving out of the balcony. The aide escorted them to the exit.

Pasturepie handed him a card as he left. "Please send me that one-pager asap."

"Will do," the aide responded.

The Magic Is Gone

The White House official walked to his sedan and told the driver to take him back to the White House, pulling out his phone to check emails and texts as the driver fired up the car.

Back in the Oval Office, Pasturepie sat in front of the big desk and told the President what had happened in the Senate. The President said he wanted to announce the details of the virus relief package at his rally. Pasturepie nodded.

Suddenly, whatever magic spell had been keeping me in the form of a tiny bug wore off. I started to grow rapidly, just as I had earlier when I knocked over the vase. This time, though, I kept growing, tipping Pasturepie's chair over backwards and sending us both sprawling onto the carpet.

The Secret Service was on me in an instant. They dragged me to my feet, arms pinned behind my back.

The President was looking at me in dull astonishment, his mouth gaping open, obviously trying to process what he had just seen.

"You know," he said, as if trying to reassure himself, and speaking to no one in particular, "I passed my cognitive test. People said it was a tough test. I had to remember an elephant, and some other things, in order, and I did it. They said it was tough, but it was easy for me. People said it was incredible. Other people, not me, but other people. Lots of them. My doctor said I did very well, perhaps the best he's ever seen."

He reached for his water glass, eyes still fixed on me. He brought his left hand over to help hold the glass but missed. The glass slipped from his right hand and hit the desk with a crash that seemed to hang in the air far longer and louder than it should have.

CHAPTER 5

Black Lives Matter

All I could think of was finding a way to stop the loud noise. It was dark. I punched my hand toward the noise in a series of sharp jabs until my fingers closed around the alarm clock.

"Damn! Still in the shelter," I thought.

I swung my feet off the cot and sat up, springs squeaking lightly. Pushing my fingers against my temples, I ran them backwards over my head, smoothing out my hair.

A wave of disappointment and anxiety swept over me. I was sure Professor Gautama's idea would resolve whatever was keeping me trapped in this dream. But here I was, still stuck in Green Valley. And my court date was tomorrow!

Was I crazy? Would I be able to keep myself out of trouble in the courtroom? If not, how would the punishment affect me?

Seeming to sense my distress, Socrates pushed his head against my knee. "It will all work out as it should," he said in his deep voice. "Just take things one step at a time. Let's get ready for breakfast."

That made sense. And I was hungry. I got up off the bed and took the dogs outside. When they had finished their morning toilet, I let them back in and left them in the dining area while I showered, shaved, and got ready for the day. I met Jesus in the dining room just before 7 AM.

"Hey!" he said cheerfully through the window from the kitchen. The smell of pancakes made my stomach rumble. "How did you sleep?"

"I slept well, thanks. No offense, but I was hoping to wake up in my home. I guess Professor Gautama's idea didn't work."

"Maybe you just need a bit more time. This is your second day in the shelter. We have some exciting things ahead today, with the Black Lives Matter protest and then President Dumb's rally. Today will be over before you know it, and I predict good things will happen on the third day. Always works for me."

"I hope you're right. I have to go to court tomorrow if I'm still here, and I have no idea what I can say to stay out of trouble."

Well, if it comes down to it, I will represent you. I have a little training in the law, and I know all the judges that matter."

"Thanks."

"Looks like some people are starting to show up for breakfast. Let's get them served."

I grabbed a couple plates and handed them to the first people in line, then kept putting plates out so people could grab them as they came through the line.

Jesus and I ate last, making sure the dogs were fed as well. Once all that was done, and volunteers were hard at work with the cleanup, we headed toward the lobby.

"I'll pull the van up front. Meet me there in five minutes. We have a meeting with the Chief of Police to get ready for our protest."

"Really? What for?"

"I'll explain on the way."

I stopped at the bathroom on the way out. The van was waiting out front when the dogs and I emerged. After letting them in the side door, I climbed into the front passenger seat and buckled my seat belt. Jesus started talking as we pulled out of the parking lot.

"Our goal is to keep this peaceful today. That takes some effort."

"We have a permit for our protest march, and I want to go over that with the Chief of Police one last time. We have made arrangements to have some Black Lives Matter volunteers along the route watching for trouble, and I want them to have the right people to contact if we need help."

"Wow! I didn't think these kinds of protests were organized like that."

"They should be. It's especially important now because we have found people try to hijack our events to make us look bad. We've even had white supremacists and neo-nazi groups join our protests in order to create violence and chaos."

"Really? How do you know they are white supremacists?"

"In the early days, they weren't very good at hiding things like their tattoos and insignia on their clothing. They are better organized now, so it is hard to pick them out unless they get arrested, and by that time they have created the scenes of lawlessness they want to create. Not everyone who shows up dressed in black is ANTIFA, and certainly not everyone who claims to be part of Black Lives Matter is interested in helping Black Lives Matter."

"That's pretty scary."

"Yeah, the real danger is that they are being helped and organized by people with bad motives. People who want to give authorities an excuse for heavy-handed use of law enforcement. So we have to be organized for peaceful, orderly protests."

"How can a protest aiming to tear down a monument be peaceful and orderly?"

"We are not going to tear down anything today. We're going to march peacefully and use our First Amendment rights to demand measures to protect people of color from disproportionate police violence, and that monuments to the Confederacy be removed. The Mayor and Chief of Police have told us in no uncertain terms that they will not let a mob pull down a statue because that is dangerous. That's a reasonable position for them to take. The Mayor is going to address the crowd after the march, and he will announce how the town intends to proceed on the issue of the statue and other systemic reforms."

"Is that going to satisfy all of the BLM people?"

"Of course not. But we are committed to a peaceful protest today. In the long run, that's the only way we're going to be heard without provoking a backlash that will destroy all the momentum we have going for us right now. So our people know we will have zero tolerance for violence. And we are prepared to ensure any violent protesters are arrested, no matter who they represent."

Jesus pulled the van into the parking lot at police headquarters. Masks on, they climbed out of the van, put Socrates and Plato on leashes, and went into the building. The desk sergeant opened a secure door that led deeper into the building, and a uniformed officer escorted them to a conference room where both the Chief of Police and the Mayor were waiting. Both wore masks.

Briefing The Plan

"Hello, Chief, and hello, Mayor. I didn't expect to see both of you."

"Hi, Jesus. It's a big day for Green Valley, between the protest march this morning and the president's rally this afternoon. When the Chief told me he was meeting with you, I thought it would be a good idea for me to sit in."

"Thank you both. We want our part of the day to be peaceful and positive. Our message is twofold: disproportionate police violence against people of color must stop, and glorification of the Confederacy has no place in American public life."

Jesus proceeded to review the plan for the protest. He started with the plan for assembly and opening remarks at Liberty Park, then confirmed the route in accordance with the permit. The march route was just over a mile and a half in length, ending at Confederate Square, a small park near City Hall that featured a statue honoring soldiers who fought for the South in the Civil War. The statue was erected in 1916. Before that time, the park had been called Mulligan Square, after an Irish pub that was still situated on a corner across the street from City Hall.

Next, Jesus went over the Black Lives Matter control plan, providing a list of volunteers who had agreed to monitor different points along the route. He asked for confirmation on the best way for these monitors to get help if they spotted trouble brewing.

The Chief was clearly impressed. He offered to have police accompany the BLM monitors to facilitate communication.

"I think we have a good plan, Jesus, but I also know not everyone wants things to go smoothly. Apart from the usual malcontents across the spectrum, in both your organization and mine, we've had reports the Fallopian Federation is inciting violent groups to disrupt events just like this. We know they used social media in the last election. We know that, in other countries, they have created the perception of instability as a pretext for their own violent interventions.

With less than 100 days before the next election, it would not surprise me to find them trying to disrupt your protest today with white nationalists, or other violent agitators. There are plenty of them in town today for President Dumb's rally."

Thank you, Chief. I think it would be a great idea to colocate some of your people with our monitors. And we will be on the lookout for agitators of any description."

"Mayor, at the end of the march, we have reserved time for remarks by you, and then by Congressman McFowler, if you will be so kind as to introduce him."

The Mayor said he would be honored to introduce Congressman McFowler, thanked Jesus for working with city officials on today's events, and expressed his confidence that their cooperation would make the day a success for Green Valley.

As they walked out of police headquarters, Jesus said, "We should go directly to Liberty Park from here. We'll just have time to talk with our volunteers before things get rolling."

Once they were all back in the van, Jesus started the engine and drove the short distance to Liberty Park. He pulled into a small pay-for-parking lot across the street from the park.

"BLM was supposed to reserve a spot here for me as one of the organizers."

One of the lot attendants came over as they all clambered out of the van.

"Hi, I'm Jesus. BLM was supposed to have paid for my parking already."

The young woman checked her clipboard and nodded.

"Yep, here you are."

She checked his name off on her list and handed him a pink 5-by-8 parking validation card to display on his front dashboard. Jesus thanked her, and they all walked across the street towards a knot of people clustered by a bandstand in the center of the park. An hour before the protest was scheduled to start, there were already about fifty volunteers present.

Keeping It Peaceful

Jesus grabbed a megaphone and addressed the group. "Hey, everybody, thank you for volunteering, and for being here early. I just came from a meeting with the Mayor and the Chief of Police, and I want you all to know they support what we are doing. Our part of the bargain is to ensure this stays peaceful and organized. Here are a few updates."

In about fifteen minutes, Jesus proceeded to summarize the comments of the Mayor and the Chief. He repeated instructions provided in a previous meeting for how to report agitators or people getting out of hand.

He told the volunteers to be on the lookout for foreigners or people from hate groups causing trouble. He asked if anyone had questions. There were none. He concluded by telling everyone to stay positive, enjoy the event, and to move to their assigned positions along the route.

There were still forty minutes or so before the scheduled start. Jesus moved to the starting point for the march and climbed up on a big flat bed truck that had been configured for him to address the crowd at start time. I put the dogs up in the cab with the windows down, and joined Jesus up on the flat bed.

There were chairs positioned for our use, so we sat for a few minutes until it was time to begin. Masked protestors gathered near the start of the protest route.

A small group of counter protestors carried signs displaying slogans like "All Lives Matter," "Blue Lives Matter," and even a few with the Confederate battle flag. A strong cordon of police kept these people separated from the main Black Lives Matter protest.

As time drew near for the official start of the protest, Jesus stood. Seeing this, counter protestors, most without masks, started to chant "All Lives Matter!" Jesus waited until some of the counter protesters had to pause to catch their breath, then he began to speak through his megaphone.

"Good morning, and thank you all for being here to participate in our Black Lives Matter protest march. We have three major goals today: the first goal is to use our First Amendment rights to demand our local, state and federal authorities take immediate, proactive steps to protect people of color from disproportionate punishment and use of force." There was a loud cheer from the crowd.

"The second goal is to use our rights to demand our local authorities remove the Confederate statue and rename Confederate Square." Another large cheer. This time, though, there were some "boos" mixed in from the "All Lives Matter" protestors.

"And our third goal is to exercise our rights peacefully and positively." A mixed chorus of cheers and boos greeted this last sentence.

Jesus continued, "Now I don't care if you've never seen another Black Lives Matter protest like this one. This is Green Valley—it's our town. I met with the Mayor and the Chief of Police this morning, and we are all committed to making this march a successful example for how to conduct a protest without destroying the town we are all trying to make better."

"For that reason, there are Black Lives Matter monitors along the route, and there are police with them in many cases. If you break the law or engage in destructive or unsafe behavior, you will forfeit your right to continue to participate in this peaceful protest, and you may be arrested."

"There are outside groups who have joined in protests in other towns with the explicit purpose of inciting violence and making Black Lives Matter look bad. We will not let that happen in our town, and to our event. If you see something suspicious, please find a monitor and report it."

"In closing, I want you to appreciate and enjoy your First Amendment right to express your righteous anger and dissatisfaction with your government. I guarantee that in this town, the Mayor and the Chief of Police are listening. Our Congressman is listening. Be safe, and I will see you all at the end of the march."

The crowd erupted in a cacophony of cheers and boos. A band somewhere started playing. The rope that was stretched across the road at the starting point for the march dropped. And the first group in the march order, students from the local community college, started walking. As they walked, they chanted "Black Lives Matter!" Some punctuated the chant by jabbing the signs they carried into the air.

As the crowd surged past the truck, Jesus grabbed my arm and leaned over so he could speak directly in my ear.

"The route of march is in the shape of a 'U'. We're going to take a short cut so we can arrive at the square where the statue is before the main group of protesters arrive. Follow me!"

He climbed down from the back of the truck, with me behind him. I opened the cab to let Socrates and Plato—still on their leashes—out. The four of us made our way across Liberty Park toward a road that cut across the top of the march route.

We quickly covered the ground between Liberty Park and Confederate Square. As we got to within a block of our destination, I noticed a suspicious van parked on a side street. The side door was open. A throng of rough-looking young men of all descriptions pushed towards the van. I could see a familiar figure handing out frozen water bottles and pointing towards bundles of sharpened PVC pipes leaning against the wall of the closest building.

I grabbed Jesus' arm and pointed. "That's Gladimeer Lillipootin! He's giving weapons to those protesters!"

Jesus pulled out his cell phone and quickly dialed one of his emergency contact numbers. Soon police swarmed over the area, arresting many of the men who were moving from the van towards the square with frozen water bottles and sharpened PVC spears.

We heard Gladimeer protesting loudly, "You can't arrest me. I have diplomatic immunity. And your President likes me. He likes my pictures."

One of the police officers responded, "We might not be able to arrest you, but we can sure detain you and prevent you from causing any mischief here today. And we'll see what else we can do once the judge hears what you've been up to."

I've been paying big bucks for terrorists to kill American soldiers in Afghanistan, and your President hasn't done a thing. I don't think he'll mind me helping you kill each other here at home, do you? Especially if he thinks it will help him get re-elected."

The police hustled him into a patrol car and drove away. Because of Jesus' planning and swift action, whatever plan there had been to disrupt the protest and incite violent activity never materialized. Jesus, Socrates, Plato and I continued on to the square. Jesus joined Congressman McFowler and the Mayor on the stage that had been erected for the speakers. The dogs and I stayed on the grass in front of the stage.

Elected Officials Engaged and Accountable

The Mayor drew cheers when he stepped to the podium and removed his jacket to reveal a Black Lives Matter tee shirt. He thanked those who had participated in the protest, including the police who had ensured the safety of all participants. He said this protest showed the rest of the country that people could assemble to express a grievance with their government, that government could allow and enable and listen to that grievance, and that these things could all be done without destruction, violence and disorder.

He continued, saying "Slavery didn't just end and go away at the end of the Civil War. It mutated like the cancer it was. It mutated into other forms, like penal labor systems and domestic terrorism that unjustly imprisoned and murdered African Americans. It mutated into segregation and unfair lending and housing practices that created ghettos in our inner cities, making it especially hard for people of color to rise economically in our society. It is time for our country to end, once and for all, the public manifestations of this shameful legacy of slavery."

"To that end, in consultation with the City Council, we are changing the name of this square from Confederate Square to its pre-1916 name, Mulligan Square, effective immediately. Furthermore, in accordance

with our laws, we are declaring our intention to remove the Confederate statue from its current location at a date to be determined. We have scheduled the mandatory public hearing on the removal of the statue for next Tuesday evening. The final vote on removal of the statue, and the determination of the date for that action, will be 30 days after the public hearing. Any person or group who wishes to preserve the statue on private land may submit a petition to the City Council. We ask the public to refrain from any attempts to vandalize or destroy the statue while we determine when and how we will remove it. As a matter of public safety, there will be security here until the statue is removed."

"The members of the City Council and I all realize the issue of Civil War era monuments is a sensitive issue for many people. And this statue here in Mulligan Square is not the only such monument in our community. Not all historical monuments are the same. Currently, we do not plan to remove any of the statues or monuments at Battle Creek, for instance."

"We have drafted a statement of principles that we think should guide our community thought process on these matters. That statement is available to the public on the city's web site. We think, for instance, that monuments should be left in place when their purpose is clearly or mainly historical—to indicate the positions of armies during significant actions or to educate the public about significant historical events— or primarily as a contemporaneous memorial to fallen comrades by veterans who actually participated in the fighting. We'll use this week's hearing to take comments on this statement of principles as well as to discuss the removal of the statue here behind me."

"Thank you again for your cooperation and participation today. It is now my privilege to introduce our representative, Congressman McFowler."

"Thank you, Mayor. And thank all of you who are in this Black Lives Matter rally here today. Really—I should say congratulations—because you have given America just what we needed the most. You have given America proof that our way works."

"We the people can use our First Amendment rights to criticize our society and our government and to call attention to injustice. We can do that without becoming a violent mob. In fact, that is the secret—the violence in protests has never really helped. It always provokes a backlash against the very change the protest is trying to make happen. What works—what makes government respond—is the critical ingredient of people power. People power is more effective without violence. That is what you have demonstrated here today."

"But we do not have to wait for a crisis to use people power. The most important tool we have for bringing people power to bear on our government is our elections. But for the past fifty years, participation in elections has been decreasing. If we can bring the same energy to our regular elections that we have demonstrated in this extraordinary gathering today, we will make government responsive to the will of the people all the time. We need to bring to every election the same energy we bring to protests like this one."

"Black Lives Matter!" The crowd's cheers mingled with a few boo's from counter protesters.

"I saw on facebook this morning where my conservative friends are all sharing this meme about a national baseball league pitcher who is refusing to kneel in a gesture of support for Black Lives Matter with the rest of his teammates. And he said he couldn't kneel for Black Lives Matter because, as a Christian, he could only kneel before God."

I do not question this young man's right to stand, sit, kneel or express himself in accordance with our Constitution. I do not question this young man's sincerity or his belief that his religion prevents him from kneeling—I am willing to accept his statement at face value. I do want to point out, however, that if he really believes his Christian faith prevents him from kneeling before anything but God, he really doesn't have a very good grasp of the scriptures he is supposed to understand as a Christian."

"I am a Christian. The requirements of being a Christian are pretty clearly laid out in the New Testament. There have always been people who try to twist those requirements in order to manipulate people for their own personal agenda. And there have always been people gullible enough to fall for those deceptions. But the fact is, there is nothing in the Christian faith that prevents someone from kneeling for Black Lives Matter. Quite the contrary."

"Christians believe Jesus came to redeem humankind because we were not living right. There were a lot of rules in the Old Testament for sure. There were a lot of people going out of their way to make sure everybody knew they were crossing "t's" and dotting "i's" when it came to following those rules. But the main point of Jesus' teaching and example and death—the reason we needed a New Testament—was that Christians are called to live in accordance with the spirit of God's law, and Jesus gave us an example of how to do that."

"Jesus tells us in the New Testament that the most important parts of the law are to love the Lord with all your heart and to love your neighbor as yourself. He uses the parable of the Good Samaritan to explain what that means. There was a long history of animosity and contempt between Jewish people and Samaritans in Jesus' day. When Jesus uses a Samaritan as an example of someone who is living in accordance with God's law, he is telling us that Christians are called to love the people who make us most uncomfortable. For Christians, that requirement is more important than crossing all the "t's" and dotting all the "i's" in all the rest of God's law. Jesus said so."

"The young pitcher correctly said that, since he didn't believe in Black Lives Matter, he would have been a hypocrite to kneel. He was right to be concerned to not act like a hypocrite. Jesus called out hypocrisy more than any other sin in the New Testament. By my count, in my Bible, he explicitly calls out hypocrites nineteen times and implicitly criticizes hypocrisy another seventeen times or so. Our young pitcher should have just stopped at not wanting to be a hypocrite."

"Instead, he goes on to say he doesn't support Black Lives Matter because he thinks they don't support the nuclear family. Imagine that. A white guy, maybe a descendant of the white people who sold black slave mothers and fathers and children and, for hundreds of years, denied African Americans the ability to have stable nuclear families— that guy can't bring himself to support Black Lives Matter because he is the great protector of the nuclear family.

My, my, how effortlessy our young pitcher jumped from the frying pan of concern into the fire of hypocrisy. I wonder if it ever even occurred to him how hypocritical his position is."

"By claiming that his Christianity prevented him from kneeling in support of Black Lives Matter, our young pitcher was not standing alone in support of the spirit of God's law. He was standing shoulder to shoulder with thousands of years of hypocrites. He was standing with people who use God's law as an excuse for staying in their comfort zones and for satisfying their own political and personal agenda. People who truly care about living a Christian life are called to do more than that. People who truly care about living a Christian life are called to act in support of racial justice and equality. People who truly care about living a Christian life are called to support Black Lives Matter."

"Thank you for letting me be a part of today's protest. Keep working together with local authorities, keep working together in peace to set the example for the rest of the country. God bless all of you, and may God bless America."

These comments were met with nothing but cheers. Jesus briefly announced that the the protest was now ended, and asked protesters to do their part to ensure the remainder of the day's activities remained peaceful. He joined Socrates, Plato and I at the base of the stage.

CHAPTER 6

Senator Cracker's Medal

"I packed some lunches for us in a cooler in the van," Jesus said. "Let's go eat, and then head to the rally."

They made their way back to the van. As promised, there were peanut butter sandwiches for Jesus and I, along with cheese sandwiches for the dogs. We ate quickly, washing down our meal with cool water.

Then, with the dogs situated in the back, and me buckled into the front passenger seat, Jesus started the van and drove us back onto the Green Valley University campus. He followed signs for the stadium, where President Dumb's rally was to be held. The parking lot was mostly empty, so they didn't have to park too far from the entrance.

A Rally Fit For A King

Masks on, dogs on leashes, we made our way into the stadium. At the gate, we showed passes Jesus had downloaded from the internet. I was surprised that no one had the slightest hesitation about the dogs accompanying us.

One of the aides, seeing our group, turned to another and said, "Call the kennel and see if they will bring their strays over here for the day. That will help us get our numbers up!"

The staff in general seemed stressed by what must have been a lower turnout than they were expecting. Overflow seating in the parking lots was completely empty. Inside the stadium, staff was working feverishly to remove social distancing stickers from seats. They were packing the crowd in to just a few of the sections right in front of the stage to so camera shots would make the crowd look bigger than it was.

The crowd was in a festive mood. None wore masks, and all wore tee shirts that identified them in groups that more or less aligned with Professor Gautama's analysis. There was a whole section in the center with shirts that read "God Bless President Trump," and another section next to them wearing " 'States Rights' = WHITE POWER" and "White Makes Right" shirts. Another section bore shirts with logos like "Trump-Callicles 2020", "I'm With Callicles" and "MONEY IS POWER". Then there was a section where people with "I Love My AR-15" shirts mingled with some proclaiming "My Favorite Magazines Have 30 Rounds Or a Centerfold." Throughout the entire crowd, a rather large number wore shirts that read "Just Happy to be Accepted Somewhere (Finally)", "Not My Fault I'm A Dud", and "Blame the Illegal Alien Migrant Socialist Left Wing Liberal Media (and Democrats)".

We got plenty of dirty looks and jeers for our "Black Lives Matter" tee shirts and face masks, but made it to our seats just in time. Ibetya Dumb emerged from the tunnel with another woman I did not recognize. The crowd erupted in thunderous applause. Ibetya smiled and waved and took her seat in the first row in front of the stage. The second woman peeled off and went directly to the podium.

"Well, it's almost time!" she exclaimed. More applause. "I'm Carrie Water, and in just a moment, that great man, our President, will come out of that tunnel with another great man, Banklyn Ham, and some other fine ministers from our local evangelical council. They are going to pray over our President. When they do, I want you to join them. I want you all to stand, and extend your hands to the President. We are people of prayer. Do your part, and let the President feel the power of your prayer. And now, ladies and gentlemen, the President of the United States of America!"

President Dumb entered, and the band played "Hail to the Chief." Following behind him, as promised, was the world-famous evangelical minister Banklyn Ham and other representatives of the local evangelical council of ministers. The President smiled and waved and joined Carrie Water at the podium.

"Mr. President, before you start, we all want to pray over you. Banklyn Ham will lead our prayer."

Everyone stood and extended their hands toward the President. Jesus and I stood, but with arms hanging loosely at our sides, hands clasped in front at about waist height. Banklyn Ham started praying.

"Thank you, Heavenly Father, for our great country."

"Thank you for our President. We know he is not a perfect man, and he may not be what many of us prayed for, but in Your wisdom You have given us exactly what the wealthiest seven percent of our country needed. We ask you to sooth our hypocritical discomfort at his pretense of serving the people and for helping him teach Your children to trade all the hard-won liberties enshrined in our Constitution for the false banner of protecting the unborn."

"We thank you for voters who are too ignorant of what the Constitution actually says to tell the difference between a reality television performer and a patriot."

"We thank you for believers who will believe just about anything we tell them without regard for what Jesus actually said and did."

"We ask you to keep our sheep blind, that we may lead them to pastures of our choosing while convincing them they are on the road to the promised land."

"We ask you to keep them willing to pay for our first-class ticket while they ride coach."

"And, most of all, Lord, we humble ourselves and ask you to send your spirit to move across this land, along with whatever support Gladimeer Lillipootin can conjure up this time, to make our mobbed-up, money-laundering con man victorious in November. In your Son's name we pray, Amen."

The crowd exploded in a mixture of cheers and applause, interspersed with chants that included "Four More Years!" and "Lock Her Up!" The President smiled, waved, and shook hands with all of the ministers who had been praying over him. He walked across the stage and hugged the American flag and kissed it. He started to turn toward the podium, but appeared to have a second thought. He pivoted quickly back toward the flag and, with an underhand motion, grabbed the gold tassles that hung about waist height from the red, white and blue flag. Laughing, he released the tassles and pivoted back toward the crowd, shaking his finger at the section where the "MONEY IS POWER" tee shirts were most prevalent. Then he walked back across the stage to the podium.

The other ministers filed down to their seats in the front sections, leaving Banklyn Ham standing at the podium. The crowd fell silent when he raised his hands.

"Mr. President, I am told it is my job to introduce a very special guest for a special, surprise presentation. Ladies and gentlemen, join me in welcoming the Senate Majority Leader, Senator Turtlechin M. Cracker!"

The crowd erupted in cheers yet again. President Dumb feigned surprise. Elton John's "The Bitch is Back" blared over the sound system as the Senator made his way out of the tunnel and up to the stage. As Cracker approached the podium, two aides came forward from the rear of the stage. One held a velvet folder and the other carried a dark box. At the podium, Cracker addressed the crowd.

"Thank you for that kind welcome. And thank you, Banklyn Ham, for your inspiring words. Especially the part about the sheep."

He turned to the President. "Mr. President, it is truly incredible that you are even here today."

Turning back to the crowd, he continued.

"Many of you don't realize how hard the President works, and how dangerous his job can be. Today I'm going to share with you something that has not been made public before this very minute for reasons of national security."

"Just yesterday, during a briefing in the Oval Office, the President came under attack from an ANTIFA drone."

At the mention of ANTIFA, the crowd booed loudly.

"It was a tense, life-threatening situation. Only the President's bravery and swift reaction prevented a serious catastrophe and loss of life. With no regard for his own safety, President Dumb grabbed a vase, exposing himself to the ANTIFA drone the whole time. Not in a bad way, of course. He destroyed the drone with the vase."

"Such heroism cannot go unrecognized. For that reason, with my authority as Senate Majority Leader, I am awarding the Senate Half of a Congressional Gold Medal to the President of the United States. Read the citation."

The aide with the velvet folder stepped to the podium and read the flowery citation written by Pasturepie the day before. Senator Cracker moved behind the President. He took a semicircle of gold hanging from a blue satin ribbon from the box held by the other aide, and hung it around the President's neck. Then he shook the President's hand.

"Congratulations, Mr. President." Everyone cheered wildly. Senator Cracker waved to the crowd and departed.

The President stepped to the podium, beaming broadly.

"I'm so proud and honored to get this Senate Half of a Congressional Gold Medal—the first ever awarded in the history of our country —for bravery. You know, people have said all my life I was brave. Other people, not just me. I would have liked to have gone to Vietnam, but a doctor said I couldn't go because I had bone spurs."

"I think it is obvious to everyone now, given that I have won this Senate Half of a Congressional Gold Medal for bravery, that, if I had gone to Vietnam, I would have won more medals than anyone else. In fact, I was talking to the Secretary of Defense and the Secretary of State last night, and they both suggested that, since I couldn't go to Vietnam really because of a disability, and since it's obvious I am very brave, that I should be awarded the medals I would have won if I had gone to Vietnam."

"Now these two guys, Secretary Whisper and Secretary Pompidou, they aren't just two yokels I named to my cabinet. Well, I guess actually they kinda are. But Pompidou, I mean, he says he fought in Germany. I think he was there in '87. That would have been in time for the Battle of Spaten Brau, or maybe even the Siege of Schnitzel. In any case, it's pretty obvious from looking at him that he's lost the Battle of the Bulge. But my point is, these are guys who know how to spell military."

"And it's totally their idea, and I think people are checking on it now, but I feel pretty confident that I will be getting those long-overdue medals before the coronavirus disappears, which could be any day now if enough of you stop watching the fake news and start taking hydroxychloroquine."

"There's another thing a lot of people are talking about. Really, a lot of people, people from every region of the country, are all talking about the idea that maybe I should be king. Of course, there are some processes we would have to go through, but I thought it was very interesting that these people, and I have heard this from so many people, and all of them thought it would be a good thing for me to be king. It's a very interesting idea, I thought. It could solve a lot of problems."

Some sections of the crowd cheered wildly. Others sat in numb silence. Someone, somewhere, started to chant, "King Dumb Come! King Dumb Come!"

The people in the "God Bless President Trump" tee shirt section went crazy. Some screamed, "That's what Jesus meant! Thy King Dumb Come!" Others raised their hands skyward and yelled, "It's the Rapture!"

He waved his hand toward the press section. "I am the Chosen One. Of course, you'll never hear about this very interesting idea from all the lying, nasty people at the fake news media. They will never cover how many people think this is a good idea. Maybe Fox will."

At the mention of the media, the crowd booed loudly.

When they had quieted down sufficiently, the President continued.

"Yes, me being king would solve a lot of problems. But those are problems many people don't seem to want to solve. We could maybe figure out where Celery Hinton's server is, and those missing 33,000 emails."

The crowd started screaming, "Lock her up! King Dumb Come! Lock her up!"

Well, right now I'm going to take a little break. If someone from my staff can assist me, I need a spotter so I can drink a glass of water. But I am leaving you in great hands. We have a wonderful country band, Q-Anon and the Crackpots, here to play some of their hits for you. And I'll be back for my second set before you know it."

Wild applause. "Four More Years! King Dumb Come! Lock Her Up!"

The band silenced the crowd's disjointed cheering with a chord from an electric guitar. All eyes and ears turned to the small set off to the right of the main stage where the band was set up, launching into their first tune.

"Ol' Celery Hinton had a server, Ee Yi Ee Yi Oh,"

Wild cheering as the crowd recognized one of their favorites.

"And on that server she had some secrets, Ee Yi Ee Yi Oh,"

"With a secret here, and a secret there, here a secret, there a secret, everywhere a secret secret,"

"Celery Hinton had a server, Ee Yi Ee Yi Oh!"

At this point the crowd chorused, "Lock her up!"

Jesus leaned over to me and said, "I've seen enough, why don't we get out of here. I think the music is hurting the dog's ears."

"Fine with me," I said, gathering the leashes.

Since it was intermezzo, no one paid much attention to us as we left. When people bothered to read our tee shirts, we drew suspicious glances, but we were used to those by this time. As we drew close to the van, Jesus realized he had locked the keys in the van. He handed me his cell phone and asked me to call the American Automobile Association to get someone to come help, while he looked around for something he might use to unlock the vehicle.

I connected right away to the Automobile Association, and they said they would have somebody there to help in 30 minutes.

Jesus returned with a wire hanger he had found in the trash. Straightening it, and then bending into a hook shape, he tried to push it through the lining of the driver's side door so he could hit the 'unlock' button.

I took the dogs around to the passenger side of the van to sit with them in the shade.

Suddenly, I heard a voice command, "Put your hands up where I can see them and don't move!"

A Teachable Moment

"Okay! I'm doing it!" Jesus said.

I stood up and said, "Hey, it's okay, this is our van."

There were two policemen about fifty feet from the van, both with weapons drawn and pointed at Jesus.

"Why are you trying to break into the vehicle?"

Jesus responded, "I locked my keys in the car when we went in to the rally."

"Do you have proof that this is your vehicle?"

"Yes, my employee identification badge, but it is also inside the vehicle."

I still had Jesus' cell phone. "I can call the shelter, and they can verify that we are who we say we are."

The other officer was now pointing his weapon at me. "Okay, where is your cell phone?"

"It's in my pocket."

"Get the cell phone slowly and make that call."

When I opened up the phone, the first contact number that appeared was for the Chief of Police. Jesus had programmed it into his phone for the rally, and had called it when we discovered Gladimeer Lillipootin. I decided to just call the Chief instead.

The Chief answered right away.

"Hi Chief, I am Jesus' friend Stephen. We are at the Dumb rally and locked our keys in our shelter van. Some police saw Jesus trying to break into the van and are asking for proof we are who we say we are. They have guns out. Can you vouch for us?"

"Of course, put one of them on," the Chief replied.

"This is the Chief of Police. We worked with him this morning on the Black Lives Matter protest. He wants to talk to one of you."

The first officer lowered his weapon and stepped backwards with his right foot, so he could cover his partner. "Go ahead and take the phone, Carl," he said.

Carl holstered his pistol and came toward me. He took the phone, put it to his ear, and said, "This is Officer Rodriguez."

I could no longer hear what the Chief was saying, but Carl relaxed right away. "Sure thing, Chief. Thanks. Do you want to talk to the perp... to the people from the shelter again?"

After hearing the Chief's response, Carl told his partner to stand down. "The Chief vouches for these guys. He wants to talk to Jesus."

"Okay, get your phone," the first officer said, with no hint of apology in his voice. He holstered his weapon.

Jesus slowly turned around, keeping his hands visible, and moved slowly to retrieve his phone from Officer Rodriguez.

"Hey Chief, that's twice you've saved us today," Jesus said.

Whatever the Chief said prompted this from Jesus. "Well, it's a teachable moment for sure. It would be great if you could give these guys the rest of the afternoon off. I'd like to treat them to a lemonade or a beer."

Jesus held up the phone to the first officer. "Officer Crowley, the Chief wants to speak to you."

Crowley took the phone. "Officer Crowley."

Garbled voice on the other end of the connection.

"Yes, Chief."

More garbled words.

"Okay, we'll do that, thank you, Chief."

Then, to us, "Gentlemen, I apologize for overreacting. We shouldn't have had our weapons drawn."

He turned to his partner, "We have the rest of the day on special assignment with these two. We are to bring the cruiser back to headquarters, and spend the rest of our shift with them."

"Terrific!" Jesus said. "We'll meet you guys at police headquarters in about 15 minutes."

The American Automobile Association man was just arriving. He quickly opened the van, and Jesus retrieved his keys.

I put Socrates and Plato in the back, and started to take my position in the passenger seat.

"Why don't you drive, Stephen? You have a license, right?"

"Sure. Yes, I have a license."

"I know a place near police headquarters, and would like to have a beer with the police officers, so I will need you to be our designated driver for the afternoon, if you don't mind."

"Yeah, that's cool with me. Will we have time to go over my situation tonight? Tomorrow is my day in court. You're still going to represent me, right?"

"For sure."

"I need help with directions getting to police headquarters from here."

We switched places, and I started the van. Jesus gave me step-by-step directions, and in just a few minutes we pulled into the parking lot alongside police headquarters.

Officers Crowley and Rodriguez met us at the front desk. The two men had changed into casual civilian clothes.

"We know Officer Rodriguez' first name is Carl, but we don't know your first name," Jesus said to Officer Crowley.

"It's James," he said.

"I'm Jesus, and this is Stephen."

"Nice to meet you all," James said. "Sorry again for overreacting earlier."

"It all worked out," Jesus replied. "Stephen has agreed to be our designated driver for the afternoon. I know a little place close to here and would love to buy you guys a beer. My way of saying thank you for the great coverage of the Black Lives Matter protest this morning. I assume you two were on duty for that as well?"

"Yeah, we sure were. That sounds great."

The men all walked out together, joining Socrates and Plato in the van.

As I slid behind the wheel, I said to the dogs, "Socrates, Plato, meet Officers Carl Rodriguez and James Crowley."

"How do you do," Socrates said.

"Hi," said Plato.

The officers responded as if having conversations with animals was nothing out of the ordinary.

"It's just two blocks straight ahead and on the right, Stephen," Jesus said. "Look for the DNC Saloon."

It took just a few minutes to get down the street and parked. Soon, all six of them pushed their way through swinging doors into the boisterous brightness of the DNC Saloon. If I hadn't known better, I would have thought I was on the set for one of the bar scenes in Star Wars. Music played too loudly, gambling venues of varying descriptions occupied three corners, and loud arguments about politics emanated from almost every table.

"What does the 'DNC' stand for?" I asked.

"Democratic National Committee," Jesus replied.

We found a table and took our seats. The waiter came and took the order all around. Everyone ordered some flavor of beer, even the dogs. When it was my turn, of course, I ordered non-alcoholic.

"Do you remember what Professor Gautama said about cognitive bias the other night, Stephen?"

"Sure."

"Will you share it with Carl and James, please?"

I summarized the various types of cognitive bias that Professor Gautama had presented at the seminar the night before.

"Thanks, Stephen, that was terrific," Jesus said.

The waiter arrived with our drinks, including bowls for the dogs' beers.

"Gentlemen, a toast. Thank you for your great support for the Black Lives Matter protest this morning. I know—we all know—you do not believe one race is superior to another. But all of us, regardless of our race or color, struggle against our cognitive bias, and that can make us judge and treat people unfairly because of the way they look. If we are ever to beat these tendencies in ourselves, we must question our preconceptions and the evidence we think we see. We have to build relationships and friendships and positive memories with people of all races, creeds and colors. In the long run, that is the only way we win as a society. We have to acknowledge our weakness, and apply discipline every day to adjust for it. I hope that our sharing this drink together is one small step toward that goal."

"Here, here, sir!" Carl Rodriguez said. "That's a goal we can only win one heart at a time."

"That's the secret to most things, I find, Carl. One heart at a time."

"Not to destroy a sensitive moment," James Crowley said, "but I'm having a little trouble figuring out that game over there."

He was pointing to one of the corner tables where they appeared to be playing something like poker.

"I recognize the roulette wheel in that corner, and the craps over there. But I can't figure out what they're playing at the card table."

"It's just poker, James," Jesus said.

"The way they are betting doesn't make any sense. Do they have different rules?"

"Nope. The rules are the same. But it is the Democratic National Committee Saloon. Everybody overplays their hands."

They finished their drinks. The policemen said they could walk back to headquarters and get rides home on their own. They thanked Jesus, said goodbye to all, and departed.

The waiter came with their tab. Instinctively, I reached into my pocket for my wallet. As I pulled it out, a folded piece of paper fell to the floor.

"This is on me," Jesus said, handing the waiter a credit card. He reached down and picked up the paper, handing it to me as the waiter ran the card through a machine and generated a slip for signature. I unfolded the paper and was studying it when Jesus finished paying the tab.

"What is it?" he asked.

"It's a copy of my DD214," I replied.

"What's that?"

"A record of my service in the United States' military. I was in the Army."

"May I see it?"

"Sure."

Jesus scanned the document. "When we get back to the shelter, remind me to make a copy of this for the court."

"Will do."

Socrates nodded approvingly. "I was a soldier too, you know. I fought at Potidaea, Amphipolis and Delium. In the phalanx, your survival depended on your fellow soldiers. Soldiers should understand the importance of our duty as social animals."

Jesus, Socrates, Plato and I walked out of the DNC Saloon. We climbed back in the van. I drove to the shelter. It had been a full day.

After dinner, Jesus and I prepared as best we could for my court appearance the following morning. We studied the citation for "insufficient identification of country of origin," and "insulting the customs of our country." He made a copy of my DD214 to submit as evidence. I was at a loss for how I could respond in a way that would keep me out of trouble if the judge was inclined to think like the ICE raven. Jesus didn't seem worried at all.

"Tomorrow's the easy part," he said. "That work has already been done for you, and there is no changing it at this point. Just don't ever forget what you've learned these past few days when it is time for you to do your part, my friend. Wouldn't you agree, Socrates?"

The dog lifted his head from the floor. "I think that's exactly right, Jesus. And now I think it's time for bed."

We all got up from the table and headed for our rooms.

"Thank you for your help today," Jesus said. "Get some sleep!"

Like the previous nights at the shelter, I was asleep as soon as my head hit the pillow.

CHAPTER 7

The Trial

And I was immediately back in my dream.

This time, however, I was normal size, which was nice. I was also in an orange jumpsuit, with my hands cuffed in front of me, in a courtroom, which was a bit of a bummer.

"Federal Court of Green Valley, the Honorable Judge Bonespurs presiding, is now in session."

"All rise!"

Judge and Jury

Sure enough, President Dumb walked into the courtroom and climbed onto the bench.

"You may be seated."

"Your Honor, this is the case of the United States versus Stephen, who is accused of impiety before the customs of our land, illegal immigration, and trespassing in the Oval Office."

A short, fat man I recognized as DamLow Bar stood at a table on the far side of the aisle.

"Your Honor, the Honorable DamLow Bar, Attorney Gerbil of the United States, representing the government."

Jesus stood up next to me.

"Your Honor, I'm Jesus, representing the defendant."

"What? Stephen and Jesus? You two come from the Land of People With One Name, or something? Jesus!"

"Yes, your Honor?"

"I wasn't talking to you."

"Sir," Jesus continued, "You were just introduced as Judge Bonespurs, but you are clearly President Dumb. How are we to address you?"

"Well, it's like Shakespeare said, 'A rose by any other name, could smell my feet.'"

"I don't think Shakespeare said that, your Honor," Jesus replied.

"Of course he did! The guy who took my SAT's for me taught me that!" Dumb said. "Mr. Bar, you may proceed."

The Attorney Gerbil waddled around his table and stood in front of the jury box.

For the first time, I noticed them. The jury. I saw Jerry, from Professor Gautama's office. And Red-Faced Bob from the shelter, sitting next to a guy in a polo shirt emblazoned with the logo of the Greenhouse Gas Food Factory. On the other side of Bob, a younger man wearing a shirt with the Burb's Grocery Store logo fumbled his cell phone into the pocket of his trousers. There were several women as well, including one he recognized from the Planned Parenthood Clinic protestors and another who had been one of the bartenders at the DNC Saloon yesterday afternoon. Some of the women he had never seen before. The last two seats were occupied by none other than Senator Turtlechin M. Cracker and Kit Hominy, the junior senator from Utah.

"Bad luck," Socrates whispered, "No dogs."

Opening Statements

"Ladies and gentlemen of the jury. The government will prove that the defendant just appeared on the lawn of Socrates, a resident of Green Valley. We will prove that he was unable to explain how he got here or how he could get home. We will prove that he said nasty, nasty things about our customs, and that he was apprehended while trespassing in the Oval Office after helping coordinate an ANTIFA attack."

"Jesus!" President Dumb gaped at me as if just remembering where he had seen me before.

"Yes, your Honor?"

"I wasn't talking to you."

"Does the defense wish to make an opening statement?"

"Yes, your Honor."

"Ladies and gentlemen of the jury, the defense will prove beyond a reasonable doubt that my client, Stephen, while a visitor in our community, is not an illegal alien. We will prove that he is an exemplary citizen. We will prove that he could not have been trespassing in the Oval Office because he was carried into the Oval Office by none other than President Dumb's own Chief of Staff, Paul Pasturepie. And finally, we will prove that my client is not impious, but rather that he has a lot of respect for the true spirit of our Constitution, and a great understanding of what that spirit really means."

Jesus returned to his seat, and DamLow Bar stood.

Prosecution

"Your Honor, the government calls the ICE Raven to the stand."

There was a rustling behind me, and I turned in my seat to see the ICE Raven making his way towards the witness stand. I quickly surveyed the rest of the courtroom, taking in all who had come to watch my trial.

Behind the jury box, I noticed a whole section of Republican senators. They each wore a red tee shirt with the phrase "I'm With Bitch!" on the front. There were some people from the shelter, the three professors from the university panel, Paul Pasturepie, and some people who looked like they worked at the hospital. Several people wore "I'm With Callicles!" tee shirts. Plato, Socrates and Descartes were sitting directly behind Jesus and I. Robin, from Burb's Grocery Store, was there, too. All the people wore masks.

Once the raven was on the stand, the clerk stood and swore the raven in.

"Raise your right wing and repeat after me. Do you swear to tell the truth, the whole truth, and nothing but the truth, so help you God?"

"I do."

DamLow Bar began his interrogation.

"Mr. Raven, will you tell us in your own words how you came to write the citation for which we are now in court, the citation that names the defendant as impious and an illegal alien?"

"I'd be happy to. I was on patrol, sitting on a tree branch and keeping an eye on the neighborhood near Mr. Socrates' dog house. All of a sudden, I noticed a man lying on the grass. Socrates came out of his house and sat, staring at the man for a few minutes until the man woke up."

"They started talking about how the man got there and why he was laying on Socrates' toy. It was obvious the defendant wasn't from here. And I thought he was being pretty evasive with his answers. So I flew down to interrogate him myself."

"He claimed to be an American, but I was suspicious because he criticized the President's handling of the virus, and he made some snarky jokes about law enforcement. When I asked him about his religious views, it was clear he wasn't a Christian. But then he started telling out-and-out lies about our history and our founding fathers. So I put a stop to it and wrote the citation. We don't need people poisoning minds with fake news."

DamLow Bar looked at the defendant, then back at the witness.

"Would you say it is possible he was trying to steal Socrates' toy, and you just happened to be there in time to stop it?"

"Why, I hadn't looked at it that way, but now that you mention it, it certainly is possible."

"Thank you, Mr. Raven." Turning to the table where Jesus and I sat, he said, "Your witness."

Jesus stood up and approached the stand.

"Mr. Raven, are you perfect? I mean, are you right all the time, in every thing that you do?"

"Of course not."

"Do you know what cognitive bias is, and can you explain it to the court?"

"I've heard of it, but I don't know exactly what it is."

"Let me tell you. Cognitive bias is the tendency we all have to interpret our experiences in ways that are not consistent with the most rational interpretation, often because our perceptions are distorted by our preconceptions and prior experiences."

"Multiple scientific studies have independently confirmed we are all subject to cognitive bias. We can mitigate it by seeking multiple, distinct, credible sources of information."

"If I were to present a witness whose view of the defendant's conduct is completely different from your own, would you admit it is possible that both you and the other witness have perceptions that have been affected by cognitive bias?"

"Well, yes, I guess so. I might also just say the other witness is wrong. It depends."

"Mr. Raven, how would you define a good American?"

"I would say somebody is a good American if they obey all laws, are respectful towards our flag and our traditions, and are respectful of our elected officials."

"Do you recognize the object in this picture?" Jesus handed the raven a piece of paper.

"It's a picture of a sign."

"Do you know what the symbol on the sign stands for?"

"It's the international symbol for a hospital."

"Let the record show the witness is examining Exhibit A, a picture of a highway sign bearing the international symbol for hospital."

"Can the sign itself make you well?"

"What do you mean?"

"Can you hold the sign against your body to fix a broken leg, or to cure a disease, or get rid of an infection?"

"No, of course not."

"You have to go to the actual hospital—the thing the sign stands for—to find the doctors and nurses and medicine and other things that make you well. That's where the goodness represented by the sign actually is, isn't that right?"

"Yes."

Jesus pointed at the American flag in the courtroom.

"Mr. Raven, can you tell me what that is?"

"It's the American flag."

"And what does the flag stand for, or symbolize?"

"It stands for our country. It stands for freedom."

"So, if we carried that flag into North Korea, and the people there decided they liked it and wanted to make it their flag, too, would the flag just sort of magically make North Korea free?"

"No, of course not."

"What does the flag stand for that makes us free here in the United States?"

"It stands for the Constitution, and for the people of the United States respecting and obeying our laws and traditions."

"So we can say it is not the hospital sign that makes a sick person well but the actual doctors and nurses in the hospital, using medicine and equipment. And in a similar way, it's not the American flag that makes us free, but rather the things the flag stands for: the Constitution and our communities of people living in accordance with the laws and processes enacted under that Constitution. Is that right?"

"Yes."

"What about paying the correct amount of taxes, and telling the truth in public statements, like in this courtroom, is that part of being a good citizen?"

"Yes, of course, that's part of obeying the law."

"Does it bother you to hear your fellow Americans criticize the President?"

"Yes."

"Why?"

"Well, because we elected the President. We followed the electoral process from the Constitution, and that is who we-the-people chose. So we should support him, not question him. He is our legal leader."

"You realize, of course, that if the founding fathers had thought the way you describe, they would never have criticized King George, never have had a revolution, and we would possibly still be a part of England?"

"Well, no, I mean, that was different."

"Do you know what this is, Mr. Raven?" Jesus handed him another piece of paper.

"It looks like a facebook page."

"What does it say?"

"It criticizes the President."

"President Dumb?"

"No, the president before him."

"Do you recognize this facebook page?"

"No."

"You should. It's your facebook page, Mr. Raven. Let the record show the witness is examining Exhibit B, a photo of a post on his own facebook page."

"Would you say a good citizen knows the Constitution, lives in accordance with constitutional principles, and obeys laws that are passed in accordance with the Constitution?"

"Yes."

"Are you familiar with the First Amendment to the Constitution? If so, please tell us briefly what the First Amendment means."

"The First Amendment gives all citizens the right to freedom of speech, and freedom of religion and freedom of conscience."

"Knowing that the defendant spoke out against President Dumb in a manner consistent with his First Amendment rights, and that the behavior of the defendant was the same kind of behavior that gave birth to our country, the same kind of behavior that expresses the freedom-in-action symbolized by that American flag, the same kind of behavior you engaged in when you criticized the previous president on facebook, do you still believe the defendant is guilty of impiety?"

The ICE raven was flustered, and appeared at a loss for words. Jesus paused for just an instant before turning to the bench.

"No further questions at this time, your Honor." He returned to his seat next to me.

DamLow Bar stood up. "The prosecution calls Mr. Socrates to the stand."

The chocolate lab hopped down and padded across the courtroom. The bailiff held the gate open for him as he climbed onto the witness stand, hopped up on the chair, turned to face the courtroom, and sat down.

"Raise your right paw and repeat after me. Do you solemnly swear to tell the truth, the whole truth, and nothing but the truth, so help you God?"

"I do."

"Mr. Socrates,..."

"It's just Socrates. I also have just one name."

President Dumb shook his head. "Jesus!"

"Yes, your Honor?"

"I'm not talking to you."

Bar started his cross examination. "Socrates, will you tell the court how you came to meet the defendant?"

"Sure. I guess it was three days ago now. I woke up and went outside to get a drink of water. Stephen—the defendant—was asleep on the grass in front of my house."

"Was he trying to steal your toy?"

"No, he was trying to sleep. It looked like he was having a dream or something."

"Did you try to wake him up?"

"No. I just sat in front of him and waited. It was getting light. I knew he would wake up soon. My appointment with the Queen had been rescheduled... I was in no hurry."

"You had an appointment with the Queen?"

"No, I'm just kidding about that... trying to tell the court I had nothing better to do, in a humorous way."

President Dumb interrupted. "The witness is reminded of his oath. Don't try to be funny. This is no laughing matter. Jesus!"

"Yes, your Honor?"

"I wasn't talking to you. Mr. Bar, please continue."

"When the defendant woke up, did he try to keep your toy?"

"No, he gave it back as soon as I asked for it."

"Was he acting suspiciously in any way?"

"No, he was acting confused. Apparently, I look like someone he knows named Peanut, and it took me a while to convince him I wasn't Peanut."

"Aha! Did he act like this Peanut was maybe a contact? Someone who was supposed to help him with his espionage?"

"No, not at all. He acted like Peanut was a dog he knew that looked like me. And he was genuinely confused. That's all."

"What happened next?"

"I asked him where he was from, and he was about to answer, when the raven flew down and started a big fuss. They got in a huge fight about presidents and kings, liberals and conservatives, President Dumb and the virus, and whether Stephen was a Christian. The raven did not like his answers, wrote him a citation, and flew away."

"What did you think of all that? Didn't you find the defendant's answers evasive and suspicious and even treasonous?"

"No, I think the raven overreacted. If he would have waited just a little, he would have found out, as I did later, that the last thing Stephen remembered was falling asleep at his desk in Utah. So he was genuinely confused to wake up in front of my house."

Socrates continued. "As far as his responses about the President, I don't think they were treasonous at all. I agree with him that..."

Barr interrupted hastily. "That is quite enough, Mr. Socrates. Just answer my questions please. What happened after the raven left?"

"Well, Stephen explained to me that he had no idea how he had gotten to my house. And now he had this citation to appear in court.

He asked if I had any idea how he could get home, and of course I did not. But I did suggest he come with me to see some friends of mine who I thought might be able to help."

"Aha! You took him to see friends of YOURS. That is very interesting. Who are these friends?"

"Uh, let's see... Descartes, Plato, Aristotle, and then I think he bumped into Einstein, and Immanuel Kant joined us for a bit as well."

"All foreigners!"

"I think Einstein was an American citizen."

"At the end of his life, maybe. A lot of people helped this man who winds up getting arrested for trespassing and spying in the Oval Office. Very interesting... that is all. Your witness."

Jesus stood and approached the witness stand. "Socrates, why didn't you feel that the defendant's response to the ICE raven was suspicious or treasonous?"

"Well, like I started to say before, I agree with Stephen that President Dumb has been criminally negligent in responding to the virus. His response from the beginning has been designed to serve his own interests, not the interests of the country or the people he is supposed to serve. In this regard, he reminds me of a Greek man I knew named Callicles."

Socrates continued. "South Korea and the United States had their first reported case of COVID-19 on the same day in January. By May, on a per capita basis, people living in the United States were 60 times more likely to die from the virus than people living in South Korea. Now, in August, on a per capita basis, people living in the United States are 82.5 times more likely to die from the virus than people living in South Korea. Given those facts, I don't think it is suspicious or treasonous for any American to conclude that President Dumb is a failure."

President Dumb, face scarlet with rage, pounded his gavel furiously. "You're in contempt! You're in contempt of court! I've had enough of you! You can't just come into my courtroom spewing fake news. And you, counsellor, would be well advised to keep your questions on the subject of your client!"

"Very well, your Honor."

"Socrates, did the defendant learn anything while meeting your friends that would help him get home, or help him answer the charges against him?"

"Well, you'll have to ask him, of course, but I think he did. Mostly just the fundamentals. He learned what he can know for sure, and what he cannot know for sure. Perhaps most importantly, he learned about the different ways people respond to the realm of things they cannot really be 100 percent sure of, and the consequences of those different responses. I think, like me, he has discovered the power of finding a good balance between his nature as a social animal and his unique value as an individual."

"Did you see anything in the defendant's behavior that would make you think he was a terrorist, or a spy, or a criminal, or a person with any sort of bad intent?"

"No, not at all."

"No further questions at this time, your Honor."

DamLow Bar stood up. "The prosecution calls Paul Pasturepie, your Honor."

The President's Chief of Staff scurried forward from the gallery and climbed into the witness stand.

"Raise your right hand and repeat after me. Do you solemnly swear to tell the truth, the whole truth, and nothing but the truth, so help you God?"

"I do."

"Mr. Pasturepie, will you tell the court how you first came to know the defendant?"

"Yes. I had just come back from the Senate a couple days ago, and I was sitting in the Oval Office with the President. Suddenly, and out of nowhere, the defendant fell on me or jumped on me, I don't know which. I just know I felt this great weight on my shoulders, and it was the defendant pulling me and my chair over backwards. Fortunately, the Secret Service reacted immediately. They restrained him before he could hurt me or the President."

"Did you ever, at any time, invite or escort the defendant into the White House or the Oval Office?"

"No, never."

"Do you believe the defendant intended to hurt you or the President?"

"Yes, I do."

"Why do you believe that?"

"Well, first, I guess, because of the way he just threw me to the ground or knocked me over or whatever. I mean, I really don't know how he did it, but that kind of collision isn't something you do unless you're trying to hurt somebody. And plus, it ws the second attack of the day in the Oval Office."

"The second attack? What was the first attack?"

"Well, earlier in the day, before I went to the Senate, an ANTIFA drone attacked us in the Oval Office. It came out of nowhere, lasers flashing. We were all paralyzed, except the President. He rushed over and grabbed a vase and destroyed the drone with it. It was the bravest thing I ever saw."

The President smiled broadly, pulling a blue satin ribbon around his neck until a gleaming semicircle of gold popped out and came to rest on his ample bosom. He smiled self consciously, looking at the medal and adjusting it so it was visible to all in the courtroom.

DamLow Bar continued. "Amazing! Such bravery. And you think the defendant had something to do with the first attack as well? Did you see him at all during the first attack?"

"I did not see him during the first attack, but I understand he has made statements since his arrest that lead us to believe the two attacks are connected."

"Thank you, Mr. Pasturepie. Your witness."

Jesus stood and approached the witness stand. "Mr. Pasturepie, approximately what time did you return to the Oval Office from the Senate two days ago?"

"Between 3:30 and 4:00 PM, I think. Somewhere around there."

"Your Honor, if it please the court, I have a computer image of this witness passing back through White House security as he has testified."

"Okay, counselor, this had better be relevant and not just a waste of time."

"It is, your Honor. Projection, please.... Mr. Pasturepie, this is you passing through White House security. Is that correct?"

Yes, just like I said."

"Thank you, and did you go directly to the Oval Office?"

"Yes."

"Thank you. Magnify, please. The computer operator zoomed in for more close-up view.

"Again." This time the enhanced image picked up an orange dot on the collar of Pasturepie's jacket.

"Do you know what that spot is, Mr. Pasturepie?"

"No. I have a spot on my jacket. So what?"

"Please enhance the image to the greatest possible magnification and resolution, focusing on the orange spot."

The computer operator hit some keys, and the image quickly increased in size and resolution until it was clear the orange spot was a ladybug. Then, with the final increase in magnification, the picture clearly showed that the ladybug had my face!

A gasp rippled through the courtroom.

"Mr. Pasturepie, that is very clearly the defendant's face on that ladybug. And that ladybug is on your shoulder."

"So even though there is probably no way you could have known it, you most certainly did escort the defendant into the Oval Office two days ago. And when whatever strange magic that brought him here wore off, he grew back to normal size and shape while sitting on your shoulder. That is why you did not see him coming. My client did not trespass to enter the Oval Office; he entered the Oval Office on your coat. And he did not attack you. He just happened to be in the wrong spot at the wrong time when the magic wore off."

A stunned silence engulfed the courtroom.

Jesus continued. "Now it is perfectly reasonable that you did not—perhaps could not—know that you carried my client on your back when you returned from the Senate to the Oval Office. However, at this point, I want to revisit something you said just a few minutes ago. And for these next questions, I want to remind you that you are under oath. You just testified that you witnessed an ANTIFA drone attack in the Oval Office, is that correct?"

"Yes, that is correct."

"And that you personally saw the President rush over, grab a vase, and destroy the ANTIFA drone with the vase, is that correct?"

"Yes, that is correct."

"Where is the wreckage of the ANTIFA drone, Mr. Pasturepie? Why hasn't any of this been in the news?"

"Well, you can't seriously expect the fake news media to cover anything good about President Dumb. And as for the wreckage, it is secret. Top secret, in fact. Top top secret. And we sent it to a top top secret laboratory facility for top top secret analysis. So you won't be seeing any pictures, or reading anything about this in the news, until it gets declassified, if that ever happens."

"As Chief of Staff, and as someone in the room when this attack happened, you must have been involved in securing the wreckage and sending it to the lab. Who did you assign to do this? Who took the wreckage to the lab?"

"Uh, I don't recall."

"Hmmm. You turned over top top secret evidence to someone, and you don't recall who it was?"

"Yes, I'm afraid that's correct."

"No further questions at this time, your Honor."

DamLow Bar stood up. "Your Honor, the prosecution calls Secret Service Agent Dye Ogenes."

A tall man in a tailored suit came from the gallery and entered the stand. In a now-familiar ritual, the clerk swore the witness in.

"Agent Ogenes, am I pronouncing your name correctly?"

"No sir, it is pronounced 'Ah-Jen-Ease.'"

"Thank you. Were you on duty in the Oval Office two days ago?"

"Yes, sir, I was."

"Describe what you saw immediately before you apprehended the defendant, and what happened that led to his detention."

"Well, I observed the Chief of Staff come in and sit down in front of the President. And then, all of a sudden, it was like he had a child wrapped around his neck like a scarf, and they fell over backwards together.

I rushed over, and by the time I got to them I could see it wasn't a child but a full-grown man. It was the defendant. But I have no idea where he came from. It was like he got beamed down from the starship Enterprise or something."

"Did the defendant resist arrest?"

Agent Ogenes chuckled. "That really wasn't an option. As he was starting to get up, I pushed him back to the ground and cuffed his hands behind his back. My partner was covering us. When I got him on his feet, he looked confused. He really did not resist."

"Did he say anything to indicate who he was working for?"

"No."

"Your witness."

Bar sat down, and Jesus approached the stand.

"Agent Ogenes, were you and your partner on duty the entire day in the Oval Office?"

"Yes."

"Did you witness the ANTIFA drone attack that Mr. Pasturepie described?"

"No, sir."

"Did you witness the President using a vase as a weapon to defend himself?"

"No, sir."

"Can you describe what you saw during the time Mr. Pasturepie claims the drone attack happened?"

"Well, it looked to me and my partner like a bird flew into a vase and knocked it over. We both saw something like that, but we could not find the bird afterward. The President freaked out and dove under his desk. He was yelling at us to take him to the bunker. He thought he was under attack, but he really wasn't."

President Dumb was livid, again. "Objection!" he thundered. "I object to this man saying bad things about his President!"

DamLow Bar spoke up softly, "Uh, your Honor, you can't really make an objection."

Dumb screamed, "Well, you can! And you should! Doesn't this guy work for you? Order him to stop his testimony immediately!"

Bar replied, "Uh, Secret Service works for Treasury, your Honor. And I really can't just order him to stop testifying."

Dumb, now apoplectic, "Well, take a note for Secretary McKnuckle-head to never let this happen again! Jesus!"

"Yes, your Honor?"

"I'm not talking to you!"

"And you, O'Jeans, you'd better remember who you work for if you expect to keep your job or ever get another promotion. Do you hear?"

Agent Ogenes replied, "Yes, your Honor."

Dumb turned to Jesus. "Proceed with caution, counselor. I'm running out of patience with your antics."

Jesus continued his questioning. "So, Agent Ogenes, you didn't see any drone, or any wreckage that could have been a drone?"

"No, sir."

"And you didn't witness anyone collecting evidence to send to a top secret laboratory?"

"No, sir."

"And you were in the Oval Office all day?"

"Yes, sir."

"Who do you work for, Agent Ogenes?"

"I work for the American people, sir. My chain of command is just an artifact to transmit the will of the American people to me in the form of lawful orders. For that reason, no one can make me carry out an unlawful order, like lying under oath."

"Thank you. I have no further questions at this time, your Honor."

DamLow Bar stood. "The prosecution rests, your Honor."

Defense

President Dumb looked at Jesus with a malignant expression. "Does counsel wish to call any witnesses for the defense?"

"Yes, your Honor. Defense calls Professor Karen Gautama to the stand."

Karen moved forward, took her seat and was sworn in.

"Professor Gautama, do you recognize the defendant?"

"Yes."

"Did he come to your office two days ago?"

"Yes."

"Please explain the purpose of his visit, and the results."

"He was confused about how he came to be in Green Valley. His description of the events made it sound like he was trapped in a dream, so I suggested he come to an evening seminar to address what I thought might free him from the dream."

"Did he come to the seminar, and how would you characterize his participation?"

"Yes, he came, and he presented several powerful ideas for improving our electoral processes. His ideas were well received by all three professors who were on the panel."

"Would you say the witness is of sound mind?"

"Yes, absolutely."

"Thank you. Your witness."

DamLow Bar stood. "No questions at this time for Professor Gautama."

Karen left the witness stand, and Jesus turned and said "Defense calls Stephen to the stand."

I stood up and entered the witness stand. The clerk swore me in as he had the other witnesses. Jesus approached the stand with a piece of paper in his hand.

"Do you recognize this document?"

"Yes, it's my DD214, a record of my service in the United States military."

"Let the record show the defendant is examining Exhibit C, Department of Defense Form 214."

"It says here you earned a Ranger tab, Master Parachutist Badge, Combat Infantryman Badge, Bronze Star with Combat Distinguished 'V' Device, and that your rank is lieutenant colonel, is that all correct?"

"Yes.

"Did you have a security clearance?"

"Yes, I had either secret, top secret, or top secret Sensitive Compartmentalized Information clearances during the entire 25 years I was in service, depending on the responsibilities of the specific job I was performing at the time."

"Do you have to be a citizen of the United States to get such clearances?"

"Yes."

"So you are an American citizen? Not an illegal alien?"

"That is correct. I have a passport, also, but I don't have it with me."

"Stephen, please tell the court everything you remember about how you came to be here in Green Valley, and your experiences since arriving here."

I briefly recounted my experiences since my last memories of my real life in Utah. People in the courtroom began to murmur when I recounted President Dumb's conspiracy to make himself king. When I confirmed Agent Dye Ogenes' account of the incident with the vase, and confessed that I had actually knocked the vase over myself, the courtroom erupted in a loud commotion.

"Order! Order in the court!" President Dumb hammered his gavel angrily.

Jesus continued his questioning. "So there was no ANTIFA drone, and you do not work for or support ANTIFA?"

"That is correct. I listened to Mr. Pasturepie and President Dumb come up with the story about the drone. They both know it is a lie."

"Stephen, you have to admit, yours is quite an unusual tale. What do you think it all means?"

Well, I was given a unique opportunity to actually live Descartes' thought experiment. When I woke up in front of Socrates' house, all of what I would consider my normal world of beliefs was gone. Armed only with the knowledge of my existence, I had to evaluate a world of perceptions that were quite strange to me—talking animals, uncontrolled shifts in my own form and size, people who seem willing to accept every absurd thing President Dumb says, and even people who seem willing to make him king."

"My companions on this strange journey—Socrates, Plato, Descartes, Aristotle, Kant and Jesus—presented a standard of value based on our shared nature as social animals. We accept that individual perspectives are distorted by cognitive bias, and we seek to mitigate our individual blind spots through dialogue and cooperation with others. Using this standard of value, we evaluate the world we live in and make choices to achieve a reasonable balance between what is good for us as individuals and what is good for the society as a whole."

"The excursions into the Oval Office, on the contrary, exposed a man whose standard of value is based solely on what is good for himself. He wants to be king. He lies to cover up his many faults and weaknesses. He lies to take credit where he doesn't deserve credit. He doesn't tolerate people around him whose success takes any of his spotlight."

"In Utah, we have a grove of aspen they call the Trembling Giant. The grove includes something like 47,000 trees. On the surface, the grove consists of thousands of individual trees. Genetically, however, they are all part of the same organism—they share the same root system. Now I do not deny that there are thousands of individual trees in this grove, but it is also true that the health of each tree depends on the health of the root system that they share."

"The lesson I take from my journey is that our individual achievement, success and happiness is connected to the achievement, success and happiness of all the other individuals in our society. President Dumb has used false religion and false patriotism to deceive many people into believing individual success and happiness requires excluding entire segments of society that don't think or look or act the way he wants them to think or look or act. President Dumb's approach excludes the perspectives of many Americans, and therefore increases the degree to which his policies are poisoned by cognitive bias. His policies reflect a less accurate grasp of reality than they would if he had adopted a more inclusive approach. That's why Americans are 82.5 times more likely to die from the virus than people living in countries with more rational leaders."

"Thank you. Your witness." Jesus returned to his seat.

DamLow Bar approached the stand.

"Mr. Stephen, that is the absolute craziest story I have ever heard. You expect us to believe that you just magically appeared here in Green Valley, that you have no idea how you got here, and that you were also magically able to gain access to the Oval Office, one of the most secure places on earth. That's preposterous!"

"I'll tell you what I think happened. I think you were recruited by ANTIFA, that they injected you with some kind of techno-serum, probably the same kind of technology that allowed them to infiltrate a drone into the Oval Office. Then, after the President heroically destroyed the drone, you were trying to escape and evade when the serum wore off. I think you are either an ANTIFA spy or a complete wacko, or maybe both."

Bar stared at me expectantly.

"Well?" he said.

I looked at Bar calmly. "I heard you make a statement. Are you going to ask a question? I think that's how cross examination is supposed to work."

"Do you really expect anyone to believe your obviously deranged story over the word of the White House Chief of Staff?"

"Mr. Bar, you heard a little bit of my resume a few minutes ago. I've read a little bit about you and Mr. Pasturepie. People don't trust him to tell the truth about whether he has a college degree. Frankly, I don't think either of you are qualified to question my patriotism or my grasp of reality. I'm pretty comfortable letting the jury decide who they want to believe."

"No further questions."

I stepped down from the stand and returned to my seat. Jesus stood up.

"Your Honor, the defense calls Professor Constance Tooshen."

Professor Tooshen made her way from the gallery to the witness stand. The clerk swore her in.

"Professor Tooshen,…"

"Call me Connie."

"Connie, would you please state for the court your professional title and qualification?"

"Well, I have a Ph.D. in Political Science, and I am a Professor of Political Science at Green Valley University."

"We heard Stephen testify that he overheard the President consulting members of his Administration about making himself king. Is this the first you have heard of this talk?"

"No, it was reported on the news last night, and in the newspapers this morning, that President Dumb was hinting that he should be made king at his rally yesterday. It created quite a stir in some circles. The circles of people who are still conscious, that is."

"Professor—Connie—is there anything in the Constitution that would prevent the President from becoming king?"

"Why, yes. Article I, Section IX, specifically states that "No title of nobility shall be granted by the United States: And no Person holding any Office of Profit or Trust under them, shall, without the Consent of Congress, accept of any present, Emolument, Office, or Title, of any kind whatever, from any King, Prince, or foreign State.""

"And what is the meaning of the word 'Emolument'?"

"Emolument means a salary, or a fee, or anything that bestows a profit."

"So, it would not only be unconstitutional for the President to become king, but it would also be unconstitutional for him to accept or solicit payments 'of any kind whatever' from foreign powers, including soliciting foreign governments to pay for use of properties that he owns in their countries?”

“Yes, unless Congress approves of those payments, that is certainly correct.”

“Is assistance with a political campaign considered an emolument?”

“Yes, it can be.”

“How does the Constitution describe the job requirements of President of the United States?”

“Well, the oath of the President is specified in the Constitution, and it is ‘to preserve, protect, and defend the Constitution of the United States.’ The Constitution also lists a number of specified duties or powers, like entering into treaties, appointing ambassadors and other such things.

In general, the Constitution says that the President ‘shall take Care that the Laws be faithfully executed.’ And of course, we must remember that all of these duties are set within the context of the six purposes for our government that are laid out at the beginning of the Constitution. Those are ‘to form a more perfect Union, establish Justice, insure domestic Tranquillity, provide for the common defence, promote the general Welfare, and secure the Blessings of Liberty to ourselves and our Posterity.’”

“Professor Tooshen, in your professional opinion, would you say that a President who adopts a policy that each state has to compete with the other states to buy supplies and equipment necessary to fight the virus is acting in a way that ‘forms a more perfect Union’?”

“No, I think if the states have to compete with each other for essential supplies, they aren’t going to be as unified as they could or should be.”

“And in your professional opinion, if a policy allows the spread of a virus in a way that disproportionately sickens and kills senior citizens and people of color, does that policy ‘establish Justice’?”

“No, I think such a policy is fundamentally unjust.”

"In your professional opinion, if a policy makes Americans 82.5 times more likely to die from the virus than citizens of another country, does that policy 'promote the general Welfare'?"

"No, I think such a policy does not promote the general welfare as well as we have a right to expect from the government of the United States."

"In your professional opinion, if a policy fails so badly in containing the virus that it later requires emergency expenditures that increase the national debt by a third, is that policy one that will 'secure the Blessings of Liberty to... our Posterity'?"

"No, I think a policy failure of that magnitude will place a financial burden on future generations that will constrain their resources, including their Liberty."

"So your testimony is that the policies of President Dumb's administration not only violate Article I, Section IX of the Constitution of the United States, but also effectively undermine four of the six purposes of government enumerated in that Constitution?"

"Yes, I would say so."

"Would you say that President Dumb is doing his job in a way that takes 'care that the Laws be faithfully executed'?"

"No, I would not say that. His job performance seems neither careful nor faithful to the intent of the Constitution."

"Professor Tooshen, changing the subject a bit, one of the charges in the ICE raven's citation is that the defendant lied when he said that at two of the first three United States Presidents were not Christians. Is that a lie?"

"No. The Founding Fathers were a product of the Enlightenment. Deism, not what people today would accept as Christianity, was probably the dominant religious view of our first three presidents. They all referred to benevolent providence at various times. Washington rejected religious dogmas of all types and was tolerant of the efficacy of diverse religious practices outside of Christianity. Jefferson produced his own version of the Bible, which contained the moral teachings of Jesus stripped of references to miracles and divinity. Adams called himself a Christian but did not accept doctrines commonly associated with modern Christianity. All three seemed committed to the separation of church and state. So it is certainly not a lie to say that at least two of the first three presidents were not Christians."

"Thank you, Professor. Is there anything you'd like to add to your testimony?"

"Yes, actually, referring back to your first question, people should not take too much comfort in the fact that the Constitution prohibits the granting of a title of nobility, like 'King Dumb.' If Congress and the courts fail in their duty to protect the Constitution, then it's possible a president could assume all of the powers of a king without the title. I don't think the founders ever envisioned a group of senators, confronted with a president like President Dumb, acting like a submissive flock of sheep..."

"Oooh Ah...." Professor Tooshen's testimony was interrupted by a low moan and a thud. Looking over, I saw that Senator Cracker had fallen to the floor. The courtroom erupted in a low roar of conversation. President Dumb thumped his gavel loudly.

"Order, order! Senator Cracker, are you alright?"

"Yes, your Honor, Professor Tooshen's testimony made me visualize... I guess I was just overwhelmed with... uh, patriotism, your Honor. Or perhaps I am merely unaccustomed to witnesses. I don't allow them in Senate trials, you know. No sense confusing politics with facts. Could we perhaps have a potty break?"

"I hear ya, Senator. Of course, court will adjourn for twenty minutes. I feel like grabbing me some flag myself!" Dumb thumped his gavel and rose. He descended from the bench and crossed the courtroom to hug the flag theatrically, just as he had done at his rally the preceeding day.

As the jury filed past, I heard Bob from the shelter thanking the Burb's Grocery store manager for the recent donation of food.

"I told you when you called, we didn't have any food to give you. I didn't send any food over to the shelter this week. Believe me, I know when I send a truckload of food somewhere."

"That's weird. There are all these pallets of food with Burb's labels on them. I'm certain of it."

Robin looked nervously at the two men from her seat in the gallery. When they were gone, she got up and left the courtroom quickly.

Court resumed with Professor Tooshen still on the stand. President Dumb told her she was still under oath.

Jesus stood, "Defense has no further questions for Connie Tooshen, your Honor." Looking over at Bar, he added, "Your witness."

Bar stood. "No questions, your Honor."

Jesus stood again, "You may step down, Professor. Defense calls Banklyn Ham."

Ham rose and walked to the witness stand. The clerk swore him in. Jesus began his cross examination.

"Mr. Ham, what's the difference between a Protestant and a Catholic? Serious question, not looking for a punchline. How did Christianity split into Protestants and Catholics?"

"Well, the Catholic Church became corrupt. Religious leaders were selling indulgences, and basically teaching people that they could buy their salvation. Martin Luther wrote his 95 Theses, and that was one of the major themes. So Protestants believe faith is what gets you salvation, not acts like penance or indulgences. Then there is the whole business about people being able to pray directly to God without need for an intermediary like the pope."

"Thank you. Mr. Ham, the dictionary defines a Christian as one who has been baptized as a Christian or has accepted the Christian religion. Will you please tell the court your definition of what a Christian is?"

"A Christian is a partisan for Jesus Christ, someone who is not neutral in the cultural conversation but is actively striving to live and advocate as a follower of Jesus Christ."

"Very good. So, why did God send Jesus? I mean, we already had the word of God in the Old Testament, right? So why was it necessary for God to send Jesus?"

"Well, people were living in sin."

"People are living in sin, now. They were living in sin 200 years ago, and 1000 years ago. I don't think that's why Jesus came, otherwise he'd be coming back like a termite man to a lumber yard. I mean, when Jesus came we got the New Testament, right? Like the salvation equivalent of an upgrade to Windows 10 or something. Basically that is the difference between Christianity and Judaism, right? Christians believe the New Testament adds something essential to our understanding of how to live a good life, and Jewish people believe the Old Testament is sufficient, isn't that right?"

"Jesus died for our sins. That's the point of the New Testament."

"Is that so? That is certainly the main event at the end of the Gospels. But I think the point might be more than that. In order to be a partisan for Jesus Christ, you must be quite familiar with Matthew, chapter 22, verses 35 to 40; Mark, chapter 12, verses 28 to 34; and Luke, chapter 10, verse 27. Can you tell the court the thrust of those passages?"

"Jesus is asked by the scribes and pharisees what the most important commandments of the law are, and he responds by saying that the most important commandment is to love the Lord with all your heart, mind and soul. And then he adds that another commandment is like the first in importance. That is to love your neighbor as yourself."

"Yeah! Preach, baby! There you go. And he even says that all the rest of the law and the prophets depend on those two most important things, right? But you know there's something funny about that—the first part about loving the Lord—is prominent in the Old Testament. It's the first commandment. Part of the Ten Commandments that are given in Exodus. The second part of Jesus' Great Commandment, though, isn't even in Exodus. It gets a relatively minor reference in the next book, Leviticus, and did not get equal billing until Jesus promoted it. Making 'love your neighbor as yourself' part of the greatest commandment is new. It's part of the upgraded software."

"It's like God looked down and saw people trying to apply the Old Testament and he realized, 'darn, there's a bug in the code.' They are not doing it right. So he sent Jesus down to move the 'love your neighbor as yourself' code up to the first commandment, and to give us an example of what that looks like. Jesus tells us the part about loving our neighbors as ourselves is essential in order to truly live in accordance with God's law. That is what is 'new' in the New Testament."

Jesus continued. "Who is our neighbor, Mr. Ham? The scribes asked Jesus that question right away. They realized the change from the Exodus version of the first commandment to Jesus' Great Commandment was a big deal, and they wanted to understand the upgrade. How did Jesus answer that?"

"The parable of the Good Samaritan."

"Right, so not only do we have to love our neighbor as ourselves, but our neighbors are the people we have the hardest time getting along with. And you are right, Mr. Ham, Jesus does die for our sins, but I submit that his sacrifice is simply an illustration, an example, of what God means by that new line of code. Christians are supposed to love our neighbors as ourselves even if it kills us."

"And all the rest of the rules aren't as important as the Great Commandment. That's the whole point of John, chapter 8, verses 4 to 11. A bunch of men show up with a woman they claim has sinned and they want to stone her because that's what they thought the old version of the software told them to do! But Jesus says, no, wait a minute. The one among you who is perfect gets to throw the first stone. Because if you love your neighbor as yourself, you apply the same standards to them as to yourself. And the men all leave, because none of them are perfect, and he tells the woman he doesn't condemn her. In other words, he tells all of us he is not going to condemn us for mistakes, as long as we keep trying and, oh, by the way, don't be hypocritical in the way you treat others."

"That all seems pretty simple to me, Mr. Ham. I mean, the Great Commandment is the main event for Christians. It is much easier to understand than trying to figure out that we're supposed to modify the commandments in Exodus with the 19th chapter of Leviticus. I have to say I agree with Martin Luther—the New Testament is easy enough to understand so we don't need any elaborate hierarchies of religious leaders, especially leaders who sell things they have no right to sell. There is no doubt that Jesus' message, while hard to live by, is not terribly hard to understand."

"What do you do for a living, Mr. Ham?"

"I'm an evangelical pastor. I give spiritual guidance and motivation, and I run an international relief charity."

"Looking at your income, you get paid pretty well for all that. Looks like your compensation has ranged from $600,000 to over a million dollars each year for the past ten years or so. You've been criticized for taking salaries from two nonprofit organizations, and for having total compensation greater than that of people who run much larger charitable organizations. Do you know what a broker is, Mr. Ham?"

Ham responded, "Someone who facilitates a transaction, usually because they have legal or other expertise."

"Well, we have already established that the New Testament is simple enough so we shouldn't need brokers, but that's exactly what I think you are, Mr. Ham. I think you sell a certain version of salvation to a certain type of Christian. Your version of salvation allows people to stay in their comfort zones of bias and prejudice. And once you've sold people the salvation they are comfortable with, you turn around to people like President Dumb and sell him the political support of your followers. The problem is that your version of salvation is not based on what Jesus taught at all—it's old software. What is the word for when you knowingly do something yourself that you preach others should not do?"

"Hypocrisy."

Jesus continued. "When a former president said he thought Jesus would approve of gay marriage, you pridefully said he was '100 percent wrong.' You threw out some scriptures that were not from the Gospels, and you said that people could not just choose the scriptures they wanted to follow."

"But that is exactly what you and others like you have been doing for thousands of years, Mr. Ham. You use scriptures that are not based on what Jesus taught. And you sell your personal version of comfort-zone salvation, just like those old catholic popes sold the indulgences that Martin Luther was criticizing."

"Matthew, Chapter 7, verses 15 to 20, Mr. Ham. You are a false prophet, a hypocrite, no more and no less. You bear evil fruit. And you lead a certain kind of comfort-zone Christian to support political false prophets like President Dumb who are the absolute opposite of what any Christian should support. Your witness." Jesus returned to the table where I sat.

DamLow Bar rose and approached the stand.

"Mr. Ham, in your opinion, is someone who doesn't understand what it means to be saved a Christian?"

"No."

"No further questions, your Honor."

Jesus stood. "The defense rests, your Honor."

CHAPTER 8

Closing Statements, and Three Verdicts

Do you have a closing statement, Mr. Bar?"

"Yes, your Honor."

DamLow Bar stood and moved to a spot in front of the jury. "Ladies and gentlemen of the jury. We have proven that the defendant came to Green Valley through mysterious and secretive means, that he failed to provide appropriate personal identification to a federal officer, that his answers were evasive and impious. He made a joke about whether he was saved! Yes, not only is he guilty of the charge of impiety for which the loyal and true ICE raven cited him, but he also engaged in subversive activity including marching in a protest and trespassing in the Oval Office with evil intent. Given the evidence, you must return a guilty verdict."

"Does the defense have a closing statement?"

"Yes, your Honor."

"Ladies and gentlemen of the jury, we have provided facts that completely refute the prosecution's case. Professor Karen Gautama and Socrates have both testified that the defendant has been honest about his confusion over waking up in Green Valley when the last thing he remembers is taking a nap in his den in Salt Lake City. They have both testified about his earnest efforts to find his way back to where he came from."

"The defendant himself has honestly testified about how he found himself in Green Valley, and in the Oval Office, through some power that he doesn't understand. He testified that this power sometimes changed his shape and size without his knowledge or consent, and we have provided visual evidence that the President's own Chief of Staff carried the defendant into the Oval Office. Indeed, the reason he was discovered in the Oval Office was that this power left him while he was still riding on the Mr. Pasturepie's shoulder. The testimony of Agent Dye Ogenes is consistent with the defendant's story and contradicts the prosecution's narrative."

"Ultimately, we have shown that this case is about deception. We have shown that the prosecution's claim that the defendant is part of a conspiracy is a deception. We have shown that many Christians have been deceived into believing the core of their faith is something that is not consistent with the most important commandments as taught in word and deed by Jesus himself. This Christian deception has been cynically performed in order to package and sell political clout to President Dumb, whose character and behavior is the furthest thing from deserving the support of true Christians. Furthermore, we have presented evidence that these twin deceptions are part of a larger effort to support giving President Dumb the powers of a king."

"The bottom line is this: we have shown the case against the defendant in not true in many respects. We have shown that case has been exaggerated in some respects for political purposes. There is much more than a reasonable doubt around the prosecution's misleading and dubious assertions, and for that reason, you must find the defendant 'not guilty'."

President Dumb hammered with his gavel. "Ok, well, now that's done, let's get to the verdict, and be quick about it. Jury, I want you to consider the evidence carefully, especially the evidence as interpreted for you by the Attorney Gerbil, er, I mean prosecution."

"The bailiff is going to take you all into a room, and I want you to come back with a guilty verdict in thirty minutes. Easy peasy. I have a plane waiting to take me to Lago de la Mar, and everyone knows how much I hate it when work interferes with my next taxpayer-funded golfing trip. Bailiff, round 'em up and head 'em out. Court will reconvene in thirty minutes."

As the jury filed by, I could hear the juror from Burb's talking to Bob from the shelter. "Hey, Bob, thanks for telling me about those groceries. I called over to check and we are missing a bunch of stuff. We suspect one of our drivers stole it. I am having her brought over here for questioning right away."

I looked around, but Robin was nowhere to be seen.

Thirty minutes later, the jury filed back in. Senator Cracker rose to address President Dumb. "Uh, your Honor, Ah am afraid we have a hung jury."

"How can that be? My instructions were crystal clear."

"Well, your Honor, a couple of the jurors voted against us, and we might be able to pressure them into our way of thinking, but Senator Hominy voted against us as well, and he says it is a matter of religious conviction and moral principle. We will not be able to change Senator Hominy's principles or his vote."

"Harrumpf! Well what are we going to do Bi... I mean Senator Cracker? I've got a flight to catch."

"Ah know, your Honor. If only we had the other senator from Utah on the jury, he is somewhat more, shall we say, pliable."

"Hey, that's a great idea!"

"What is?"

"Senator Cracker, get 24 of your Republican senators with the red tee shirts from the gallery, and have them break up into 12 groups of 2, and be quick about it."

Cracker turned and called Senator Graham Cracker over and whispered in his ear. Soon, twenty-four Republican senators clustered in groups of two all around the jury box. A low murmur arose with all the moving about.

Dumb hammered his gavel. "Order! Ladies and gentlemen of the jury, in order to achieve law and order, because I am the law and order judge, we are going to redistrict your jury. I want each of you to go join one of these groups of senators. One juror, two senators in each group. Got it? Go!"

A low murmur arose as they organized themselves according to the Dumb executive order.

The President hammered his gavel. "Order! Now, each group take a vote on whether the defendant is innocent or guilty, and then Senator Cracker you tell me what the verdict is."

More murmuring. Senator Cracker scuttling about. Another gavel strike. President Dumb spoke sharply, "Senator Cracker, what is the verdict?"

"Suh, the redistricted jury finds the defendant guilty!"

"I thought so!" Dumb exclaimed with glee. "I can usually tell just by looking at 'em. While we're at it, let's get the redistricted jury to vote on the contempt of court charge against Socrates the dog. In fact, let's just change that charge to Impiety! What says the jury?"

More murmuring. Senator Cracker scuttling about. Another gavel strike. President Dumb spoke sharply, "Senator Cracker, what is the verdict?"

"Suh, the redistricted jury finds the dog guilty!"

"No judge in all of history has been able to make a courtroom work as well as I have made this one work, everyone is saying it, and I have to admit, I think they are right. Now let's get to sentencing!"

"Your Honor, there is one more matter... " It was the juror from Burb's that spoke.

"Well, what is it man? I've got a plane to catch!"

"Your Honor, some groceries were stolen from Burb's Grocery Store and delivered to the Green Valley shelter, and we think the thief is that woman right there!" He pointed to the rear of the courtroom, where Robin, cuffed and in an orange jumpsuit, was being led in.

"You, there, what's your name?" Dumb barked.

"I am Robin Hood," she replied.

"Did you steal groceries from Burb's Grocery Store?"

"Yes."

"Senator Cracker, do we need a verdict from our jury? You heard the confession with your own big, turtley ears."

"Well, your Honor, to be perfectly proper, we should…"

"We're a long way past perfectly proper, Cracker, but have it your way. Just be quick! Daddy's got 18 holes with my property manager from Moscow!"

More murmuring. Senator Cracker scuttling about. Another gavel strike. President Dumb spoke sharply, "Senator Cracker, what is the verdict?"

"Guilty, your Honor!"

"All right, now for sentencing. You have all been found guilty, so therefore…"

"Uh, your Honor, excuse me," Jesus interrupted.

"Jesus!"

"Yes, your Honor?"

"What do you want?"

"Oh, well, I was just going to tell you, before you get too far along with the sentencing part, that you can't actually punish Stephen. You have to punish me for his ah,… alleged, crimes. Those are the rules."

"What do you mean, those are the rules? This is my courtroom, and I am the judge!"

"Yeah, this is your courtroom, and you are the judge, but I'm Jesus. And you have to play by my rules."

"And what happens if I don't play by your rules?"

"Do you have any idea how many golfers get hit by lightening every year? Nobody is gonna even blink if there's one more at Lago de la Mar tomorrow."

Then he said something in two languages I didn't understand. The words sounded like "Tay Punya-my-ush? Ca-peesh?"

"Well, if you put it that way. And all I have to do is punish you for the crimes we convicted Stephen for?"

"Yep."

"No!" I cried.

"Do the dog first," Dumb said. "Bring in some hemlock water! Quick!"

"No!" I cried."

"And these two, Jesus and Robin Hood, crucify both of them right away!"

"Get Marine One fired up and don't forget my clubs!"

"No! You can't do that! Stop! I won't let you!" I was yelling as loud as I could and trying to move my arms. But all I could do was shake my shoulders. My shoulders were shaking. The courtroom was gone.

Karen was shaking my shoulders. "Wake up. You fell asleep at your desk again. Sounds like you were having a nightmare."

ABOUT THE AUTHOR

Stephen Tryon published his first book, *Accountability Citizenship* (A Toolkit for Information-Age Citizenship), in 2013. *Thy King Dumb Come* is his first published fiction. Mr. Tryon served in the United States Army, and his military awards include the Ranger Tab, Master Parachutists Badge, Combat Infantryman Badge and the Bronze Star Medal with Combat Distinguished "V" Device. He is a businessman, technologist, and former Senate Fellow, with degrees in Applied Sciences, Computer Science, Philosophy and Information Systems. He lives in Salt Lake City, where he enjoys hiking, traveling and time with family.